ARCANE SPIRIT

THE DARKLAND DRUIDS - BOOK TWO

NICOLE R. TAYLOR

Arcane Spirit (The Darkland Druids - Book Two) by Nicole R. Taylor

Copyright © 2020 by Nicole R. Taylor

All rights reserved.

This book is written in British/AU English.

No part of this book may be reproduced in any form or by any electronic or mechanical means, including information storage and retrieval systems, without written permission from the author, except for the use of brief quotations in a book review.

The Banks O' Doon (Second Version) by Robert Burns, cited with permission under fair use via Project Gutenberg.

www.nicolertaylorwrites.com

Cover Design: Pixie Covers & Nicole R. Taylor

Edited by: Silvia Curry

1

The Warren was still, and all through the tunnels nothing stirred—not even one of Delilah's mouse constructs.

I sat underneath *Salle*, the grand willow tree which grew inside the central cavern, watching as it shimmered underneath the crystal ceiling. Her weeping branches floated in the air, some trailing upwards, others down, giving the otherworldly impression of a million-armed octopus swimming in the sea.

"Isn't she a pretty thing?"

I looked up at Rory, glad he remembered to meet me. It *was* three a.m., otherwise known as the witching hour, and I wouldn't have been surprised if he'd fallen asleep.

The young Druid sat next to me on the snarled tree root, his ruddy brown hair sticking up at odd angles. His clothes were in a similar state, but considering the hour, I couldn't blame him for not dressing up.

"I don't think I'll ever get tired of looking at it," I replied. "I miss it."

"Speaking of missing things…you missed Burns Night," he declared. "It was a good one this year…on account of everyone not dying and all."

"What's Burns Night?" I asked, ignoring the last part. Some things still struck deep and I wasn't sure I'd ever get over them. Fighting the Chimera singlehandedly and dragging them all into death with a dangerous dark power wasn't something one did flippantly, let alone dealt with like a throwaway scene in a movie.

"Robert Burns, the poet," Rory declared. "We celebrate his birthday."

I made a face. "I'm guessing that's not a Druid thing."

"Ach, no. It's a Scottish tradition. We love our poets, especially Mr. Burns." He winked. "You know, sometimes I feel more like a Scot than a Druid."

"You certainly sound like one."

"I've lived underneath Edinburgh in a crystal cave locked inside a pocket of space and time my entire life," he said with a smirk. "Doesn't get any more Scottish than that."

I shook my head and chuckled. "So, what do you do on Burns Night?"

"Eat, drink, sing, and read poetry."

"Read poetry?" I couldn't imagine Rory reading a poem, let alone performing one.

He shook his head incredulously. "Have you read a Burns' poem? I think not!" He leapt up onto one of *Salle's* thick roots and proclaimed, *"Ye banks and braes o' bonnie Doon, How can ye bloom sae fresh and fair; How can ye chant, ye little birds, And I sae weary, fu' o' care!"*

"Don't yell," I complained. "You'll wake everyone up." I stood and tried to grab his flailing arms but my laughter stopped when my hands passed right through him.

Reality rushed to slap me in the face as my smile faded and I stared at my palms. For one blissful moment, I'd forgotten where I was.

You left to protect them, I told myself. *It was for the best.*

"Don't fash yourself, Elspeth," Rory said, jumping back to ground level. "It's not ideal, but we still get to see one another. That's something, right?"

"I'm using an unstable dark power to astral project into the one place I shouldn't. I—" I clamped my mouth shut as I felt tears prickle in the corners of my eyes.

"You left all your things here."

I sniffed. "I know. I had to buy new underwear."

He laughed. "See? It's not so bad, huh? Wherever you are, they have department stores."

"Some people would consider it a travesty of modern consumerism gone wild. The environmental impact alone—"

"Don't be dramatic." Rory chuckled and glanced up at *Salle*. "I know your da was a scientist——"

"*Environmental* scientist."

"Environmental scientist," he corrected himself. "But there's no need to be dramatic."

"Maybe if there were more Druids, then we could take on climate change."

Rory chuckled. "Wouldn't that be a sight? How would we ever explain it to humanity?"

I sighed. There wouldn't be any environmental soldering while the Warren was besieged by the Chimera.

"It's been a while since I last checked in," I began. "How are things?"

"A month," he replied. "A whole month."

"I…" My cheeks heated and I looked away, wanting to hide behind the curtain of green hair. The hair that marked me as half Fae. *Half enemy*.

Rory shifted so he could catch my gaze. "I should be asking how *you* are. The Druids can handle themselves just fine, but how long has it been since you found out the truth?"

"Three months." *Though it felt like three thousand years*. The learning curve was steep and the price of being special was high. Half Fae, half Druid.

"And it wasn't an easy transition," he added, "not by a long shot. Your da passed away only a month before you came to Edinburgh, too."

"Have the Chimera returned?" I asked, not

wanting to talk about my adjustment period or my father being murdered by an elemental soldier.

"The city has been quiet," he replied. "There are still Fae around, but not like it used to be."

"Good." They were all out looking for me just as I'd planned.

"You're safe, though?"

I nodded. "I think so. I haven't seen any Chimera for a while."

"Are you sure about not telling me where you are?"

"Yes."

"Your powers?"

"I...I've been too afraid to use them much," I admitted. "I've only practiced a little at a time."

"A little is good," Rory said. "I mean, you're astral projecting like you've been doing it for years. That's not exactly a Druid ability."

I offered him a half-smile. "I guess not."

Sitting back—which was an odd sensation when I couldn't feel my arse—I thought about the night I'd confronted Owen and the Chimera in Calton Cemetery. He'd said a lot of things to me that night, but I'd pried his truth out like a parasite latching onto a blood vessel.

The Chimera wanted to take over the Fae world, then sweep into Earth, destroying the witches for barring their way home, enslave the Druids, and when they had the power they desired, they would turn on humanity.

The Chimera wanted to rule with a dynasty of terror that stretched across multiple worlds. They wanted to become all powerful…and they needed me in order to achieve it. If Owen was to be believed, then my mother held a similar ability to the one I'd discovered that night —and they'd tried to turn her into something evil against her will. She'd fallen in love with my father somewhere along the way, but when I was born, I'd inherited the Druid power to open portals between worlds as well. Thus, I'd prompted an ominous prophecy to be foretold.

Born of ashes, dead in darkness, a soul who bridges the gap has the power to destroy Druid and Fae alike. When the black sun rises, death will choose the hand of fate.

If anyone bothered to ask, I'd tell them that prophecies sucked.

"Stop worrying about it," Rory declared, sinking down next to me. "It is what it is."

He was right. Sulking wouldn't change anything.

"How's Ignis?" I asked. "Keeping his promise?"

Ignis was a rather large tabby cat, but he was more than just another mouse catching feline. He was a complex construct made from Druidic prisms that housed a broken human soul. It was my grandmother Delilah's favourite pastime. She said saving shards of people destined for an eternity of nothingness and shoving them into magic cats was a better fate than anyone could hope for.

But when it came to Ignis's soul, there were more questions than answers. Firstly, he'd somehow grown a mind of his own and began to act like a bratty teenager, ignoring my pleas to stay inside the Warren where it was safe. Secondly, he'd turned himself into a giant tiger with glowing blue stripes and launched himself into battle beside me. It was kind of bad-arse, but no one could explain it. His level of consciousness was unprecedented.

"He hasn't disappeared, if that's what you mean," Rory replied. "And he hasn't changed into anything else but a lazy fleabag who sleeps in the library all day. He still chases the bird constructs, but he hasn't managed to catch one yet."

"Good to hear."

"He knows you're okay."

I grunted, still unaccustomed to the attention of other people. Growing up, I'd always been a loner with nothing special to write home about.

"What have you been doing?" I wondered. "Still patrolling with Jaimie?"

"Yeah, but...I've been trying to perfect my portals," Rory admitted. "Everyone has a speciality, except for me. I thought it was about time I got one of my own. Wandering around Edinburgh and spying on Fae wasn't exactly something for younger generations to aspire to."

"You're a warrior," I told him. "A *neach-gleidhidh*." A guardian. "That's something great to aspire to."

"Maybe." He shrugged. "Portals are useful too, even if I can't open them to other worlds. There aren't many of us who can control them."

"Be careful," I warned, thinking about my father.

His meddling with portals led him to the Fae realm, my mother, and everything that'd followed. It was the reason the Darkland Druids were hunted by the Chimera.

"One day I might find the Darklands," Rory said. "But for now, other worlds are far beyond my reach."

"Still—"

"Elspeth, it's all good," he interrupted. "I know you're worried, but I'm being careful. I know what I'm doing."

"If you say so…"

He shook his head. "I trained you, didn't I?"

"It still won't stop me from worrying."

"*Yes, Mother.*"

He meant it as a joke, but I tensed. Rory's parents had been killed by the Chimera soon after my father returned to the Warren with me, a mere three-day-old baby, in his arms. I couldn't help but feel partially to blame for the calamity that'd followed in our footsteps, even though I had no control over it.

We fell into an uneasy silence until Rory cleared this throat.

"Vanora—"

"I don't want to talk about your genetic girlfriend," I huffed.

"She's not my girlfriend. Besides, I can't help it if tradition dictates that in order for our genetic survival, we have to—"

"Please stop," I snapped. The Druid's dwindling

gene pool was just another reminder that I'd never truly belong anywhere. No one wanted my sullied blood mingling with the pureness of Druidic kind, regardless of my grandmother being an Elder or anyone's feelings otherwise. It was never going to happen, so it was better to not become attached in the first place.

"Elspeth, they want to apologise, especially Vanora and Darby."

"Apologise?" I scoffed.

They'd accused me of leading the Chimera to the Warren, attacked and restrained me, then tried to justify killing me while bound to *Salle* with prisms which burned into my flesh. If it wasn't for Delilah, Darby would have plunged a knife through my heart. Still, I'd gone out into the city and protected them all by unleashing the monster inside me, risking the fulfilment of their stupid prophecy.

When the black sun rises, death will choose the hand of fate.

"They understand what you did for us," Rory continued, "everyone does. They know they were wrong. The Darklands rejected us and we're not without our faults because of it, but—"

"Well, I'm not ready to forgive them for attempted murder," I hissed and rose to my feet. I no longer bore the wounds from the attack, but the emotional ones still ran deep. "I unleashed a demon to save them. How stupid am I?"

"*Elspeth.*"

"I can't," I told him. "It's too much. I need… *I need silence.*"

I let go of the threads which bound me, and my essence snapped back into my body. I opened my eyes, grabbed the pillow next to me, smooshed it into my face, and screamed.

The cottage was dark and silent, save for the echoes of my frustration and the howling wind over the hills outside.

I hadn't ended up far from Edinburgh, but it'd been a long road to get here. Instead of going south to London, I'd gone north to Inverness. Even in the snow and ice, the Chimera had followed, but I'd managed to disappear before they could lay eyes on me.

Rattled, I'd gone rural, phasing onto the banks of Loch Lomond.

I'd found the notice by chance, happening on it at the village grocers I'd stopped in looking for a hit of chocolate—the farther I teleported, the more drained I felt. The advert had gone something like, *McDougall's Trossachs Hobby Farm is looking for short-term help over the winter. Accomodation provided and fair wages supplied.*

As it turned out, it was a young couple with a daughter who were just getting the place up and running. They knew only slightly more than I did about farm animals, which wasn't much. After a few uneasy glances at my green hair—because unnatural hair colour was a sign I might be of the rebellious sort —we'd come to an agreement. I stayed in the single level, stone cottage free of charge and received a little envelope with money stuffed inside, all in exchange for collecting eggs, herding cows, a bit of milking, and a whole lot of shovelling shite.

I couldn't complain too much. The cottage was cozy and wired with electricity, the family was nice, it was isolated, and the scenery was beautiful. If the Chimera found me here, it'd be a miracle.

Still, I had to be careful with using my abilities. It seemed like they could track me somehow, as if using my powers was the same as firing off a flare gun in the wilderness. Astral projecting seemed to be okay so far, but I wasn't going to push it by helping the herb garden sprout out of season.

I sighed and tossed the pillow away, the dark cottage suddenly cold. Now I knew why Dad never used his Colours. I'd only known about my own for a few months, but I already missed practicing prisms and turning on and off crystal light bulbs with a wave of my hand.

Unfurling from the couch, I shuffled over to the window and pressed my forehead against the cool glass. Outside, the stars were shining through a break in the clouds, glittering like diamonds strewn across black velvet.

How had my father coped with this life? Constantly looking over his shoulder, always with a lingering threat of death or worse snapping at his heels? Cut off from the one thing that made him who he was. How had I been so blind to it all?

There was a darkness inside me, but it was more than my Druid legacy to walk into death or my still-unknown Fae heritage. Once I'd let the darkness in that night at Calton Cemetery, something had spoken to me. Something wild and elemental…and beyond this reality.

I had no idea what it was or why it had chosen me. All that was certain was that I couldn't let the Chimera get their hands on me.

Because if they did…it was all over.

2

———

The weather was a strange beast in the Scottish Highlands.

I leaned back from the window, rubbing my nose where it'd gone numb from leaning against the cold glass.

Summer was just around the corner, but it still felt like the cold fingers of winter were clutched around the wooded glens, braes, and lochs of the Trossachs National Park.

The most famous loch in the area was Loch Lomond—Loch Ness, with its famous monster, was three hours to the north—and if I stood at the front door of the cottage, I could see a sliver of shimmering water peek through the treetops.

I shivered, my conversation with Rory playing in my mind. There wasn't much to see outside at this hour of the morning, so I sat on the couch and pulled a handwoven blanket over my legs.

I picked up the black bag Delilah had given me at the train station in Edinburgh and took out my father's journal. I hadn't opened it yet as courage had been in short supply since I'd left the city.

Facing my father's death and being a Druid was one thing, but dealing with the darkness that came with my mother's lineage was an entirely different ball game—one I wasn't sure I wanted to play.

The journal was heavy in my lap, the worn cover cool to the touch. Tiny scratches and dents marred the leather and the binding was creased. Whatever was inside must have been important—Dad had opened it often, it seemed.

Delilah had told me it contained his portal research, and I'd assumed it was full of equations and insights to the places he'd been while searching for the Darklands. Maybe there were a bunch of portal addresses…if that was even a thing.

"Okay, Dad," I murmured, "I know I went into death and spoke to you, but I can't avoid the things you left behind forever."

Before I lost my nerve, I unwrapped the leather tie and flipped open the cover.

The paper was thick, as if it'd been handmade out of recycled pulp. Flecks of wood fibre ran through it, creating an interesting mottled effect, but it was the writing inside that held my attention the most. A rush of unwanted feelings bubbled to the surface and I almost closed the journal.

I ran my fingertips over Dad's familiar

handwriting, tracing the curves and angles. I swept the pages over and found more of the same. He'd used different kinds of pens—felt-tipped fine liners, grey lead pencils, biros—in an array of blacks and blues. Some notes were scribbles while others were neatly written thoughts. There were drawings, too.

Runes were etched in corners or doodled as he'd been lost in thought. I recognised some of the shapes from around the Warren. That one was for light, another was nature, night, day, sun, and moon, but there were many I didn't know. Rory hadn't taught me much about languages before I'd left, but there was an understanding that lingered in my blood that caused me to find many of the shapes familiar. It was how I'd finally managed to realise what Vanora's favourite insult—*bò bhrònach*—meant.

I'd stood on the platform, about to get on a train to London, when understanding flooded my mind. It was what made me go north, with the hope that I'd one day return to the Warren. If only she knew calling me a stupid cow would have such a major effect on my trajectory…

Shaking my head, I turned back to the first page and began to read what my father had felt so deeply about that he'd wanted to commit it to paper.

I remember flashes of the Darklands. A colourless, crystalline world; a nightmarish barrier between Thrìbhís Mhòr and countless other realities.

Mother suspects Merlin made a pact with the Old Ones to conceal the homeland from outside threats. They would wrap

Thríbhís Mhór within the Darklands and our way of life would be safe from those who followed us through space and time. The price for their protection was the souls of the unworthy. That's what she thinks, but Merlin would never admit it.

If that was true, then by rights, we shouldn't have survived.

Merlin? I snorted. Stranger things had happened than finding out an old wizard dude from fictional stories about King Arthur actually existed.

Unworthy. I recalled something Rory had said to me when we'd first met. It was in the safe house on the Royal Mile after I'd first met Vanora. *There are those amongst us who believe we aren't worthy of reaching the homeland,* he'd said. *Vanora is one of them. I fear it's turned her heart hard.*

It must be difficult knowing they escaped a fate they'd been destined for, especially knowing their leader, Merlin, had made a bargain to sacrifice them without their knowledge.

I didn't like the connotations of the Darklands deeming someone as 'unworthy'. It made the Darkland Druids sound as if they were tainted in some horrible, irreparable way, and all they were good for was becoming shadow people in a nightmarish world. *No wonder Vanora was bitter.*

I continued through the journal, but it was mostly scraps of notes complaining about lack of progress. *Portal opened to Borneo. Portal almost dumped me into the Atlantic Ocean. Portal went nowhere. I'm having trouble finding a connection to realities outside this one.*

Rory told me portals were difficult to master and that it could take a lifetime to find a path to another world. No wonder Merlin had monopolised the way to the homeland. *Pfft.* I hoped for his sake, we never met.

On the next page, Dad's writing became messy.

I found a path to a new world, he wrote. *My Colours have finally broken through the veil of our new Earth, and I looked upon the face of another…the first I've seen in hundreds of years. It was bright and full of life, a stark comparison to the Darklands.*

I gasped and read the passage again just to make sure I wasn't jumping to conclusions. Dad had been amongst the Druids who'd escaped the Darklands.

My heart hammered in my chest and I stared across the room, completely numb. My father had been over eight centuries old when he'd come to Earth.

Holy…

And in all that time, he'd never loved anyone else or fathered any other children. At least, none that Delilah mentioned. I was it. Just me and him.

I frantically searched through the journal, skipping pages and entries, scanning for mentions of my mother or the Fae world, but it wasn't until I reached the end that things became interesting.

A few pages had been ripped out, the jagged stumps were all that remained, but there was one last entry. Dad had written only a few words and drops of water had smeared the ink, but their meaning was unmistakable.

I can't control what I feel for her. It has overtaken me. I love her.

That's when I realised it wasn't water, it was tears.

There were no notes about the Fae realm, what it was like, who my mother was, why he'd taken me and ran. It ended abruptly, as if he knew writing about it would be dangerous.

I flicked through the rest of the journal anyway, only to find empty pages.

If only we had more time… But that was my curse, apparently. Questions were answered with more questions and an unhealthy dose of regret.

Sighing, I let the journal fall back to the last entry.

I stared at Dad's admission of love—and the tears which stained it—and wondered what it was like to feel that intensely for someone.

In that moment, I felt a stab of loneliness so profound I didn't know what to do. Sniffing, I pressed my palm against the page and the cottage fell away into darkness.

Whispers echoed around me and I spun, trying to catch them, but no matter how hard I tried, or how fast I turned, they slipped through my fingers and dissolved into the currents of time.

A vision collided with me and I gasped. I stood in a forest, feeling the warmth of a strange sun on my face. A beautiful woman peeked shyly around a tree, her emerald hair shimmering as she moved, but her face was a blur.

I blinked, my heart leaping into my throat and time sped up.

Her hand was in mine. Her hand *was* mine.

An icy chill tickled the back of my neck and I turned.

Snow lay thick on the ground, sparkling in the dim light.

I stood in a stone room on the edge of the world.

My hand reached for the curtains, but it wasn't my own.

"Gordan?" a woman called, a note of distress in her musical voice. "She comes."

I turned, snatching up a leather bag and dragging the strap over my head.

The small, round room was lit with candles, the orange glow illuminating the stone walls with long shadows. Bookshelves dominated the space, and each shelf was crammed full of curiously bound tomes in a rainbow of colours. Tapestries had been hung in empty spaces and long velvet curtains draped either side of the open window.

"Can I trust you?" I asked, startled to hear my father's voice. I was witnessing his memories.

A woman lingered in the doorway, wringing her hands together. Her features were feline—sharp cheekbones, strong yellowish eyes, and golden hair that fell around her shoulders and down her back.

"They will know," she replied. "But I will try to stall."

"Thank you."

A fourposter bed materialised from the haze of memory—a massive thing with a thick fur blanket. I leaned over and scooped up the swaddled child and held her tightly against my chest.

She never made a sound, choosing to sleep her way into a new world. I couldn't blame her.

The sound of a squalling baby echoed through the castle as the harvest moon covered up the sun, turning the land grey and black.

"The black sun." It was a woman's voice, different than before, distorted by eroding memory.

"I don't care," I said in my father's voice. "Our daughter is here." I looked down upon the child, smoothing away the gunk on her perfect little face. "Have you ever seen something so small?"

"You don't understand…" the woman said.

Looking at her, I replied, "I understand perfectly."

I knew she was there, lying in a bed of strange furs—tousled, exhausted, and radiant. But I couldn't see her clearly. She was a phantom.

"They will covet her power for the rest of her life," she said.

"And we will protect her for the rest of ours."

I tore my hand away from Dad's journal and I stared across the cottage, disoriented and a little nauseous. *Mother.*

The sounds of the Scottish Highlands came back

piece by piece—the rustle of the wind in the bushes outside, the drip of the tap in the kitchen, the creaking of the old wooden beams in the ceiling—and my wits returned, along with the feeling in my fingers and toes.

It was a world like ours but with a layer of magic over it so thick, it tasted like honey.

I shook my head and closed the journal, wondering what part of me had linked to Dad's memories. I listened to the dawn, but all was still.

Delilah was right. The journal *did* hold a clue that only Gordan's daughter would understand.

And it broke my heart and mended it, all in the same breath.

3

A furious rapping at the door woke me.

I jerked upright as if someone had tossed a bucket of ice water over my head. I snorted and blinked the sleep out of my eyes, I tossed aside the blanket and rubbed my aching back.

Dad's journal fell onto the floor with a thud and I snatched it up, shoving it into my bag before I got sucked into any other memories. Whatever happened last night, I now had an annoying headache that throbbed behind my eyeballs.

"Elspeth? Hello?" The child's voice was muffled on the other side of the heavy, wooden door.

It was the McDougalls' daughter, Florence. At seven years old, she was a tenacious little thing with a fearless attitude—though fiercely shy around strangers. Her curly brown hair was often tangled with bits of twigs and leaves stuck in it, and her favourite outfit was a red tartan shirt, jeans, and wellington boots—wellies for short—so she could slosh in the mud to her heart's content.

I opened the door, the overcast sky a little too bright for my overtired eyes. The girl stood on the path, wide awake and full of beans. She looked up at me with a little awe and a whole lot of admiration, though I suspected she thought I was cool because my hair was green, not because of anything I'd done.

"Hey, Florence," I said. "How are you this morning?"

"Da's lost a cow," she replied, pronouncing cow as 'coo'. "He told me to come ask if you'll help look for her."

The McDougalls kept half a dozen of the iconic Scottish highland cows, lovingly referred to as 'hairy beasties'. They were lumbering, longhaired, shaggy things with rather large horns, though they were quite placid and leisurely creatures. The bull was a deep, almost black-brown, but the ladies of the little herd were all ginger beauties.

"Her?" I asked. "It's not Harriet, is it?"

Harriet was my favourite. She was the smallest, cutest, and shiest of the crew. Perhaps I saw some of my own qualities in her. *Elspeth Quarrie, relating more to a cow than a human being.* Seemed like something I'd do.

The little girl nodded. "Aye, she didn't come with the rest this morning."

My knowledge of cows was rather lacking, but I did know that they loved to follow things. If Harriet got separated from the herd, she wouldn't come back to the farmhouse on her own. We'd have to go out there and bring her back.

"Okay. Well, give me a minute to get my boots on and I'll go look. Are you coming?"

"Aye," the little girl said, beaming up at me. "Da said I could if it was okay with you."

I smiled and nodded. "Of course. I'd be glad for the company."

Leaving the door open, I shuffled back into the cottage and rustled around in my bag for the ibuprofen tablets I always carried around with me—a staple in my everyday survival kit. Headaches were the worst, especially when there was nothing around to take for it.

Looking over my shoulder, I saw Florence waiting outside. She was balancing on the stone edging around the garden with her arms stretched wide.

Grabbing the knife Rory had given me out of my bag, I strapped it to my waist and pressed my palm against the hilt. A drop of Colour warmed my palm and spread over the blade, shimmering it into invisibility. I doubted I needed it out here on the side of a rugged hill, but I wasn't taking any chances, especially not with Florence in tow.

I tossed back the headache tablets, chasing them with a gulp of water, and shoved my feet into my boots. Stomping outside, I closed the cottage door and waved to Florence. "Ready?"

Florence jumped off the stones and landed with a

flourish. "Da said to look in the top field. That's where the cows like to go the best."

I looked up at the steep hill and already felt the burn in my thighs. "Well, we better get going."

The morning was clear, yet brisk, and we began the long walk across the farm with Florence humming a cheerful tune. It sounded like the latest pop song to top the charts, but I wouldn't know what it was. I'd lost contact with the human world the moment I'd met Rory Mackenzie.

I snorted. *Human world.* It hadn't taken much for my view of the world to change.

The gates between the fields were open, and our boots squelched in mud as we passed over the well-worn trails. Hopping onto the stubby grass, we made our way farther up the hill.

Florence's father, Richard, told me that the grass didn't grow much because of the weather and landscape. The Highlands used to be covered in glaciers which eroded the soil over time, so now grass and plants grew wherever earth had gathered in the rocky ground. Red deer and sheep grazing tended to strip a lot of it, too.

The grass grew well enough on the farm, but he still liked the herd to come back to the sheds to feed, especially in the winter.

"What is the weather like in Australia?" Florence asked.

"Well, it's not like here," I replied. "It's dry most of the time and very hot. Where I lived, we got lots of rain and storms, and in the summertime, it was so hot, sometimes the trains couldn't run because the tracks bent."

"The trains don't work here in the winter sometimes," Florence said, chatting happily. "They get all icy. Do you get snow?"

"Not in Sydney, but there are mountains where people can go skiing."

"Wow. I thought Australia was a desert. Is it true you keep kangaroos as pets? My friend Agatha says you walk them around on leads like dogs and they have pouches you can put things in."

I burst out into laughter and shook my head. "No, we don't keep them as pets. They're wild animals." The imagination of children never ceased to amaze me.

I helped her over the stone fence and into the top field, following with an ungraceful roll over the top of the rubble that sent Florence into fits of laughter.

Rory's knife was heavy against my side and the illusion I'd woven to conceal it tingled a little as I righted myself.

"I meant to do that," I declared, much to her amusement.

The ground was rugged here and rolled up and down, creating miniature glens and dales. Harriet could be lingering in any of them, just out of sight. We'd have to walk one end to the other, much to my dismay. My thighs were aching already.

It wasn't long before I spotted Harriet's ginger

head in the distance and I heaved a sigh of relief. The cow was very much alive and upright.

"There she is," I said, pointing across the field. "Stay here, okay?"

Florence nodded and picked up a stick and began whacking the grass. Harriet was a placid beastie as befitted her breed, but if something spooked her, her horns had the potential to do some serious damage.

As I approached, a mess of discarded rubbish caught my eye and I cursed under my breath. Someone had taken it upon themselves to dump a bunch of twisted wire and metal in the field, tossing it over the fence from an isolated dirt track in the dead of night, rather than take it to the local council tip— if there was such a thing around here.

Harriet was standing beside the mess, her breath vaporising on the air as she chewed on her cud. I held out my hand for her to smell and looked into her dreamy, chestnut eyes.

"Hey girl," I murmured, stroking the soft hair on the bridge of her nose. "We were worried about you."

When I was satisfied she was calm enough, I rounded her flank, trailing my palm over her side so she'd know where I was. I'd been taught how to move around horses as a kid and a cow didn't seem that different…except for the horns.

Seeing the problem, I clucked my tongue. Her shaggy hair was caught in a knot of discarded barbed wire and the sharp prongs had torn her flank where she'd tried to free herself. Blood matted her side, but the cut wasn't too bad. Though we would have to call the vet once we got her back.

"Oh, Harriet," I murmured. "What a mess you've got yourself into. You're more curious than a cat. Why people dump rubbish where it can hurt animals is beyond me. Lazy sods."

The cow mooed forlornly, calmed by the press of my hand on her flank. My Colour soothed her thrumming heart and I reached for Rory's knife, glad I'd brought it along.

"Keep still, okay? I've got to cut you free."

I rasped the blade over the tangled hair, cutting away the wire piece by piece. I wondered what Rory would say if he knew how I was using his precious Druid knife. Runes shone faintly along the length of the metal, declaring a prayer to the homeland, Thríbhís Mhór.

The last of the wire fell away, I rubbed my palm over the cut in the cow's side.

"There," I said. "We better get you back to the others. Unfortunately, there's going to be a visit from the vet, but it really isn't that bad. *Promise.*"

I felt the presence of the Chimera immediately and my head snapped up as a terrified scream echoed across the field.

Florence.

Forgetting about Harriet, I sprinted across the paddock, almost slipping on the dewy grass.

A man loomed out of a dip in the field and I came to an abrupt halt. My gaze moved from the man to

Florence. He held her against his legs with a knife at her throat and his other hand over her mouth.

Chimera.

The little girl's eyes were full of tears, her fear palpable.

"It's going to be okay," I told her. "Don't move."

"It's time to come with me," the Chimera said, his face flickering between his illusion of humanity and the greying skin of the Dark Fae he truly was.

"How do you keep finding me?" I demanded, even though I knew he wouldn't answer. It couldn't have been the minuscule amount of Colour I'd used on Harriet, it—

The journal. I cursed under my breath.

"Either you come with me now or the girl dies," the Chimera said. "It's your choice."

"You say it like there isn't a third option," I drawled.

"There is no third option."

"*I beg to differ.*" I allowed my grip to loosen on the darkness imbedded inside me. "Dragging innocent children into your evil plans for world domination is the last straw. You people just don't get it, do you? I'm not for sale. I'm not to be bargained with. *And I'm not going with you.*"

I blinked and my vision darkened, blurring as my power took hold.

Lifting my hands, I squashed down the fear that rose in my heart as I saw the familiar black liquid ooze out of my flesh from my first knuckle to the tips of my fingers. It hissed and spat as it hit the ground, eating away at the grass like acid.

Where the grass burned, fissures opened like pits of tar, opening the way for the otherness.

Just the Chimera, I told the shadow. *Protect the girl.*

The ground tore up in front of me, carving a vicious path towards the man. He let go of Florence with a startled cry as the liquid wrapped around his ankle. It dragged him away from Florence with a violent tug, tossing him ten feet into the air. He landed across the paddock with a sickening crunch, but I knew he was still alive—Chimera didn't die so easily.

"Elspeth!" Florence shrieked, falling to the ground.

"*Run and hide*," I cried.

She sobbed but didn't complain once. She wailed as she began to run, limping and hopping across the field.

I clutched Rory's knife and strode towards the Chimera as he scrambled to his feet. He held his side as he swung around.

"Where's your magic, Fae?" I rasped, my voice not entirely my own. "You're weak away from your world, aren't you? Do you want to go home?" I slashed at the Chimera, the knife cutting through flesh.

He recovered quickly and stabbed at me with his blade, a spark of unfamiliar power pushing the knife through the air.

I twisted to the side, dodging the blow like Rory

had taught me in one of our many training sessions back in the Warren. Spinning, I smashed the hilt down into the back of the man's neck.

He collapsed in a heap, rolling onto his back. I straddled him, the darkness taking control of my limbs, and sneered down at my prey. His illusion had completely melted away, leaving his true face bare to the sky.

Sickly, greyish skin, beady eyes, and pointed teeth —a man, yet a monster within.

They wanted to hunt us? the shadow hissed. *They know nothing.*

My hands curled around the Chimera's neck and squeezed, the ground disappearing beneath us. The black ooze devoured the earth and crawled over the Chimera's flesh, dragging him downward…but I didn't give in to the deeper force of possession within.

"I don't fear death!" he cried, clawing at my hands. "You will be our saviour!"

His fanatical words gave me pause, but the shadow ignored his blind faith, instead relishing the easy defeat of the Fae.

The black essence crawled over his face, thick veins spreading and growing until he was choking on the congealed ooze. What was it? After all these months, I barely knew. Negative energy? Black blood? Tar? Oil? It had no smell, nor could I feel it. It was nothing and everything.

The Chimera gave one last gasp, his breath

bubbling as the liquid essence sucked him into the earth and swallowed him whole.

I gasped as my hands passed through nothing, then slammed into the ground. The ground, with its stubby green grass and jagged glacial rock.

The black ooze—and all traces of the Chimera— was gone.

"Florence?" I called, the shadow lingering in the back of my mind. "He's gone. You can come out now."

She emerged from within a little hollow and rushed towards me. Throwing herself into my arms, she cried, scared out of her wits.

The darkness rushed towards her and I held my breath, pushing it back down with everything I had.

Not the girl, I told it. *We care about her.*

You care about the girl?

Do you care about anything, shadow? Is suffering so beautiful to you? More than the sky, the earth, the animals, magic…love?

It didn't reply.

Have you learned nothing from me? I asked it.

The shadow hesitated, then subsided, merging with me once more.

"It's okay. He's gone." I held onto Florence as she cried, soothing her as my skin turned pink with warmth. "He can't hurt you anymore."

"The m-monster…" she sobbed. "H-he…"

How in the world was I meant to explain this to her *and* her parents?

My Fae blood rippled, twisting around my Colours as if it were trying to tell me something. *Calm her and make it go away. No child should live with the memory of a monster.*

So that's what I did. I rubbed my palm on her back and told her a story, weaving my words with a power born to me from another world.

We'd found Harriet and, in our excitement, Florence had fallen and hurt her ankle.

"I didn't mean to fall," the little girl said, wiping at her tears. "It was an accident."

"I know. You won't get in trouble, but you might have to go to the hospital and get an x-ray."

"The h-hospital?"

I smiled and nodded. "It's not scary, I promise."

It was ironic, really. The only thing that'd been holding me back was my fear. I knew my heart and now, so did the darkness.

I glanced to where the Fae had stood and sighed. "Wanna hop onto my back? I'll carry you home."

Florence nodded, wiping her sleeve over her snotty nose. I helped her up and squatted so she could wrap her arms around my neck and grasp my waist with her legs. Even though I felt a little drained from the fight, I managed to stand without falling.

"You're so brave," I told her.

"I am?"

"You're as brave as my dad," I replied. "And he was a firefighter who rescued people from humungous bushfires."

"Really?" she whispered into my ear.

"*Really.*"

Finally, we fetched Harriet, who came when I called, responding warmly to the flow of my Druidic Colour. Then, we made our way back to the farmhouse, a morose parade of broken things.

4

———

When we got back to the main farm, we left Harriet in the yard outside the shed and made our way to the house.

Florence was heavy on my back and my poor thighs screamed in unison with my shins and what felt like blisters on all my toes.

Richard was wheeling a wheelbarrow out of the vegetable garden when we rounded the side of the cottage. Florence wailed at the sight of him and he came running, almost knocking his load of weeds over on the path.

"Florence!" He lifted the girl off my back and cradled her in his arms. "What happened?"

"She fell in the top paddock and twisted her ankle," I said. "I brought her back straight away."

"I'm sorry, Da," she sniffled. "I didn't mean to fall."

"Don't worry, lass," he told her as the front door

of the house flew open and Florence's mother—Annie, who was a perfect grown-up copy of her daughter—barrelled across the yard.

"Florence! Oh, my sweet girl." She extracted her from Richard's arms and fussed over her.

"I don't know what we would have done if you weren't there," he said to me. I'd been worried they'd blame me for being careless, but kids were meant to play in the dirt and get bumps and scrapes. Just as long as the Chimera remained a secret, then everything was good.

"Don't worry about it. It was an accident," I said. "It could have easily been me or someone else tumbling in that hole."

"We have to get her to the doctor," Annie said. "Just to make sure nothing is broken."

"My leg is *broken*?" Florence cried.

"No, probably not, but the doctors have to check," she replied. "I've got to take your boot off, okay?"

They hurried inside and Richard turned to me. "Did you find Harriet?"

"She got stuck on some barbed wire," I said with a nod. "She's got a nasty cut on her flank that'll need to be seen. People have been dumping scrap metal in the top field again."

"Ach," he cursed. "It's becoming a real problem. Thanks, Elspeth."

"She's in the yard. I didn't want to touch it incase she spooked." A pained cry from Florence dragged my attention back to the house. "Is there anything I can do?"

"No, don't fash yourself. Annie'll run her down to the local GP, though he might just tell her to go to the hospital in Alexandria. It could be a long day."

"I can wait for the vet if you want to go with them?"

"That's okay, Florence will want me to take care of Harriet. She loves those cows and God forbid if anything happened to them."

I laughed and shook my head. "I wish I had a drop of her conviction. I always wonder where it goes when we grow up."

"Don't we all."

Sometimes being a grown-up sucked. Reality and responsibility took away all the magic…even from those who had access to the real thing.

My smile faded as the remnants of the darkness tingled in the back of my mind. "Okay, well I'll finish off my chores. If you need anything, I'll be around."

"Thanks, Elspeth."

I gave him a wave and wandered across the yard towards the chicken coups. Picking up the basket from where it hung on the fencepost, I eased through the gate and into the pen.

Chickens and ducks began to quack and cluck, circling in the hopes I was about to feed them.

As I checked for eggs, I finally had room to breathe and decompress after the fight on the hillside.

The Chimera knew where I was. If I didn't leave,

they would try again. The McDougalls would be in danger and next time, Florence might not be so lucky.

This place had felt like paradise, but it was just the eye of another storm.

I knew they wouldn't come after me straight away, especially after what I did to that Chimera. He was alone, which meant when he didn't report back, someone would need to come looking.

I had a day, maybe two, to get myself in order. Where would I go next?

Maybe tomorrow, when I'd had time to recover some energy, I'd phase someplace else to create a false trail, then get a train or a bus to another city where they couldn't trace me. I'd lay low until they caught my scent, then repeat the process all over again.

I'll be running for the rest of my life.

I closed my hand around a warm egg and pulled it out of the nest, laying it in the basket with the others I'd collected. Kneeling in the muck-covered straw, I lost myself inside my dilemma.

I could believe living a life one step ahead of the enemy was my only option, but this was the life I'd *chosen* that day in Edinburgh. I'd stood on the platform outside the door of that train with two options. Get on or go back to the Warren. I wound up on another train, but I still had chosen to leave.

I picked this.

I wanted to take all the burden because I believed I didn't have anyone who would miss me...but that wasn't true. I had Rory, Jaimie, Ignis, and Delilah.

If I kept running, was I really solving anything?

Something pulled on my hair and I cursed as I swatted away a duck who'd mistaken my green locks as a strange new variety of lettuce.

It was hard to admit, but as I knelt there amongst the shite-covered straw, I knew I'd picked the cowards option.

I'd chosen to run when I should have stood up and fought. Now I was too afraid to go back. I'd just witnessed the price of battle and it was too high. A child's life had been threatened all because of me.

Elspeth Quarrie was no longer a nobody. She was worth the future of an entire world.

I was exhausted when I returned to my little cottage on the edge of the property. The sunset was beautiful that night, stretching orange, red, and purple fingers across the sky.

After hosing the chicken shite off my boots, I pushed open the door and stomped on the mat, kicking off the last of the grit and water.

That's when I saw Ignis.

He was curled up on the couch, nestled in the blanket like he just wandered in and claimed the place as his own. His outstretched paw lay on the cover of Dad's journal—the same journal I was positive I'd put into my bag that morning.

"Ignis? *What in the world…?*"

The robust tabby cat lifted his head and yawned, showing me all his teeth and then some.

"How did you get here? You couldn't have walked all the way from Edinburgh." I hesitated. He could change into a tiger…maybe he flew? His fractured human soul couldn't have that much control over his Colour-constructed body, could it? "What is it about you?" I wondered out loud. "You just keep showing up like a stage-five clinger."

He purred and narrowed his eyes in that contented way cats had when they were overly happy about something. He thought he was clever, that much was obvious.

"Well, you're just going to have to go back," I said, sitting beside him. "A Chimera found me this morning. I killed him, but there'll be more. He…he attacked Florence, the daughter of the farmers who live here. *A seven-year-old child.*" I sighed and pet Ignis on the head. "I can't be responsible for people getting hurt like that. I have to move again, and you have to go back to the Warren."

Tomorrow, I decided. I'd go in the morning after I said goodbye to Florence and thank the McDougalls. I owed them that much—just disappearing would be heartbreaking for the little girl.

A knock sounded on the door and I patted Ignis on the head. "Be quiet, okay? I wouldn't know how to explain you."

He meowed and looked at the door, his tail swishing.

Sighing, I got up and opened the door to find Richard standing on the stoop, the last of the sunset fading in the sky behind him.

"Oh, hey," I said. "Is everything all right?"

"I just wanted to thank you again for today," he told me.

I narrowed my eyes, sensing something a little askew about him. Maybe I was overreacting after letting my darkness out, but I'd learned the hard way that I needed to trust my tingly supernatural sense. I wasn't about to let my guard down now, not when I knew my location had been outed.

Deciding to go fishing, I asked, "What did the butcher say about Harriet?"

Richard smiled. "He'll get some good cuts off her. Paid well, too."

Paid well? The real Richard would *never* sell Harriet to be slaughtered. *Ever.* Florence would be heartbroken, and that little girl was his entire world.

I kept a straight face and allowed a trickle of my Colour to come forth. I knew what he was without feeling the chill that came with their presence, but like a sadist who enjoyed pain, I had to see for myself.

His illusion flickered, revealing the inevitable and I sighed. *Chimera.*

I was so sick of them. Sick and tired. *Exhausted.* It'd only been three months, and I was already at my wits' end. How did Dad deal with it for twenty-five years?

Ignis had turned up just at the right moment as

always. He was like a herald of change and a beacon of strength, just when I needed it. I guessed it was time to change my mind.

"Richard would never sell Harriet to the butcher," I stated, glaring at the Fae.

Fake-Richard smirked. "You can make this difficult or easy, Elspeth."

"It's always difficult with me, I'm never going to change. You really need to stop asking because I detest repeating myself."

"Then so be it."

"Before we begin, just tell me one thing." I held up my hand to stop him from reaching for the sword I knew he had concealed with an illusion. "Were you Richard all this time?"

The Chimera chuckled. "You tell me."

There was no way to be sure and the a-hole knew it. I was too blind to the ways of the Fae and the supernatural to understand if there was a difference between the Richard who stood before me now, and the Richard who I'd worked with on the farm these past two months. The Druids knew how to hide, and so did the Chimera.

However, I *was* smart enough to know he was alone—a simple scout looking for a lost soldier—but he wouldn't be for long. Their response time was improving.

"I don't have time for this," I snarled, lunging for him.

He didn't have time to react as I wrapped my arms around him and phased.

The dark, choppy waters of Loch Lomond appeared below us and we fell, hurtling towards the surface. The Chimera cried out and I shoved him away, trying to extract myself from his flailing arms.

We tumbled over and over, and I pushed a burst of Colour towards the Fae, blasting him loose, then phased the hell out of there before I could hit the water.

I landed face-first with a thud, the air whooshing out of my lungs. Gasping, I held my side and pushed to my knees, desperately dragging oxygen into my body. *I really have to work on my landings.*

Blinking, I realised I was in the garden outside the McDougalls' farmhouse.

Rising, I pushed down the pain stabbing in my side and dragged myself across the grass to the house. *I had to know.*

The backdoor had a window set into the wood panelling, and I peered through the glass. Richard and Annie were on the couch with Florence bundled in a blanket between them, watching the latest animated kids' movie on their television.

So the Fae was just using his face after all. I heaved a sigh of relief at the same time I feared the Chimera, who was currently swimming back to shore. I had to be gone before the Fae made it.

Richard spotted me lingering outside and I

jumped, lifting my hand to knock in a lame attempt to cover my creepy spying.

I grimaced as he opened the door, warm air spilling out into the night.

"Elspeth," he said looking me over, "is everything all right?"

"Yeah, I just wanted to check on Florence. I was worried."

He glanced over his shoulder and stepped outside with me. "It's a bad sprain, nothing that won't heal given a little time. She'll have to use crutches for a few weeks, but it's already a huge game. I thank God every day for a giving us a lass like her. Nothing fazes her."

I flinched slightly at the word 'faze'. "Oh, that's great. I'm glad."

"Thank you for being there with her. I don't know what would have happened if she'd fallen up there alone. She does like to wander."

Guilt tugged at my heartstrings and I managed a half-smile.

"Are you sure everything's okay?" he asked again. "You don't seem yourself. You've, uh…" he plucked a twig out of my hair, "you've got a little something caught there."

"I, uh… I actually came to tell you that I have to leave in the morning. I know its last minute and unexpected, but I, uh… I have a friend who needs my help and…"

"Oh, that's a shame. Is there anything I can do?

Do you need a ride into town?" If he only knew what really happened this morning, he wouldn't be so quick to offer, but the fact that he offered at all was a testament to his character. Most people would've immediately asked why.

I shook my head, anxious about the floater I'd left in the loch. If things weren't so dire, I'd probably be laughing my arse off right about now. It was one of my finer comedic moments.

Richard frowned, but accepted everything I said without further pause. We were technically strangers after all. I mean, how well could you know someone after a few weeks of shovelling cow shit together?

"Do you want to see Florence?" he asked. "I know she'll miss you."

"In the morning," I replied. "It's been a big day and I don't want to upset her."

Richard regarded me for a moment, then smiled. "You're a good person, Elspeth. We're really going to miss you around here."

"Ditto."

5

———————

Standing in the centre of the cottage with my bags slung over my shoulders, I picked up Ignis and held him tightly.

The cat looked up at me with a judgemental expression.

"I know I suck," I said. "It's better this way. If I say goodbye to Florence, it'll break her heart. She'll forget about me easier this way."

Ignis narrowed his emerald eyes.

"*Stop.* Anyway, I don't have time. That Chimera would have made it back to shore by now. We have to jump or fight it the dark way." I shivered. "I don't think I can handle another dose of negative energy. It really zaps my..." *Will to live.* I swallowed hard. "Ready?"

I hadn't phased with anyone before, not until I'd dropped the Chimera into Loch Lomond. I wasn't sure how Ignis would take it being a construct and all, but he didn't appear worried. He purred, pressing his cheek against mine, his disapproval over my ghosting Florence forgotten.

I thought of the Warren, picturing its magical turquoise and black walls in my mind, then made the jump.

I landed, my startled gaze falling on Rory and Vanora. I was in his room inside the Warren, and they were... *They were kissing.*

My cheeks heated as they tore apart and stared at me in startled surprise.

"Elspeth?" Rory whispered.

Panicking, I focused on the first place that came to mind.

Library, library, library.

I phased, landing amongst the familiar display cases and bookshelves. Ignis yowled and leapt from my arms, scurrying away. I suppose he decided he wasn't a fan of teleportation after all.

"Oh my goodness."

I turned to find Delilah sitting on a couch underneath the amethyst dome, clutching her heart. She wore her usual crocheted vest over a loose linen shirt, a dozen rings on her fingers, and a tangle of beaded and crystal necklaces strung about her neck.

"Elspeth, you scared the Colour out of me," she said, rising.

At the sight of her, I burst into tears and dropped my bags. The flood of emotion was unexpected, and I threw myself into my grandmother's arms, glad I finally had someone to ugly cry in front of.

"I couldn't do it," I managed to choke out. "I tried, but they kept finding me. They attacked a little girl to try to get me to go with them. *A child.*"

She smoothed my hair. "The Chimera know no limits to their cruelty."

I cried for a full minute before I could gather myself. Delilah just held me, saying nothing. I didn't want to admit to her that I was wrong about leaving, let alone the pang of jealousy at accidentally interrupting Rory and Vanora, but my presence was enough.

"Dad… How did he do it?" I asked once I'd caught my breath. "He hid me for twenty-five years before they caught up with us…and I couldn't even last three months."

"Gordan was a highly skilled Druid, Elspeth," Delilah said, drawing back. She smoothed my hair away from my face, her Colour dancing across my skin as she swept away my tears. "He had centuries of understanding. No one expects you to match him, especially not after a few months." In other words, don't be so hard on yourself.

"I had to let the darkness out to save Florence and it almost took her with the Chimera. Delilah, I—"

"Shh," the Elder murmured. "You did what you needed to. Nothing more."

"*I rewrote her memories.*"

She hesitated, her expression turned thoughtful. "Another mystery."

"There's too many of them and they all have dangerous consequences."

"Well," she declared, "at least you have the good sense to know your abilities come with an ethical dilemma."

I stared at her. "I thought…"

"You thought I'd be worried?" She took a deep breath and guided me to the couch.

"My control. I—"

"*Can* you control it?"

"Yes, I seem to be able to, but—"

She pressed my shoulders to make me sit. "You paint yourself to be a monster, Elspeth. You call the power inside you dark, but the Druids believe that no power is truly evil, only the one who wields it is."

"Choice?" I whispered.

Delilah nodded. "Yes. Choice is what makes us who we *truly* are."

"But I don't understand. The Chimera want to force me to the darkness."

"They can force you, Elspeth, I'm not denying that. But they cannot change your truth." She set her palm over my heart. "*Your* soul will forever be your own. No one else can ever touch it, no matter how much they try to force you."

I didn't realise I'd been holding my breath, and I let it out in one long whoosh. They might end up forcing me to destroy their enemies and raze the

Earth, but I would still be Elspeth in *my* soul. Just mine. The way Delilah spoke told me no one else had the ability to protect themselves like I did merely through birth. If anyone knew, it would be her—the collector of broken things.

Was it another aspect of my mixed blood or a link to the prophecy that bound me to two different worlds? Maybe I'd never know.

"I think I understand now," I murmured. "As well as I'm able to anyway."

"Elspeth, I'm glad you've returned, but…" She took my hands.

"But?"

"The Druids have always been a peaceful people," she told me. I got the feeling she was skirting the truth. "We exist in harmony with all things, nurturing and guiding. We were never warriors."

I sighed. "Not until my father brought the Chimera down on us."

"No, not then."

"What do you mean?"

"As you know, we travelled to many worlds and settled on an Earth much like this one. Darkness came for us then. *True* Darkness, Elspeth. Creatures born of the hatred of the stars. *Manifestations of choice.* We learned to fight in order to return home. We became warriors then, but for us, those who have become known as the Darkland Druids, we put our weapons down the day we decided to make our home here.

When the Chimera came, we were unprepared and I fear we still are."

"What are you saying?" I asked with a scowl. "You can't fight with me? Or you won't?"

Delilah smiled, pleased with my fiery answer.

"*Delilah.*" Rory told me older Druids could be vague with their answers—it was all about the journey and finding my own way to them—but this was next-level.

"We've forgotten how to fight, but your return means we have to remember." She could have said that straight up, but it would have been too easy…and coherent.

I groaned and slapped my hand against my forehead, finally getting it. "*Choice.*"

I'd chosen to come back to the Warren and that could only mean one thing. *The prophecy.* The soul who bridged the gap between the Druids and the Fae had chosen to side with the Druids…and now it was time fight.

The Elder beamed. "*Precisely.*"

"I could still change my mind," I warned, saying it more to rebel against destiny than actually meaning it. "The black sun hasn't risen yet. Or at least, I don't think it has."

"Maybe," she said in a sing-song voice. "Are you hungry? It's past dinnertime."

Dinner? After everything we'd just talked about, she was thinking about food?

The library door crashed open and Rory rushed in. "Elspeth? Are you in here?"

I groaned and closed my eyes. *Colour preserve me.*

"Trouble in paradise?" Delilah asked.

I opened my eyes and scowled. "What paradise? I accidentally phased in on him and Vanora tongue wrestling. That horror is burned into my retinas for all eternity."

The Druidess chuckled. "Oh dear."

I didn't want to think about what I'd phased in on, let alone talk to Rory about it. I imagined his lips were still smeared with Vanora's lipstick. *Gross.*

Elspeth, you're a grown-arse woman. Get it together.

"I'll have to discuss your return with the other Elders," Delilah said, glancing at Rory. "For now, settle in best you can. You're safe here, but when it comes to matters of the heart, I'm afraid I'm of no use."

"It's not like that," I complained, my cheeks flushing.

She chuckled and rose, her jewellery clacking together. "If you say so…"

"Elspeth?" Rory's voice came again.

"Over here, Raurich," my grandmother called. She turned to me. "Be gentle, granddaughter."

I snorted as she disappeared, leaving me and Rory alone in the library. Where Ignis had vanished to was anyone's guess. That cat had the right idea and I wished I could disappear with him rather than have a conversation with Rory right now.

I shoved away the image of the Druids kissing and cursed. After all the times we'd spoken since I'd been away, he never once mentioned that he was hooking up with Vanora. What did I expect, though? They were genetically matched to perfection and he didn't owe me any explanation.

I didn't want to admit that I was a little too attached to him—even though we could never be a thing because, you know, *genetics*. Not that Rory saw me that way.

Ironic that when I thought about home and the Warren, my subconscious had phased me straight to Rory. *More like irritating.*

Hearing his approach, I stood. I'd only astral projected a few nights ago but seeing him in the flesh was suddenly awkward.

"I didn't mean to intrude," I told him briskly. "Sometimes I land a little left of where I'm aiming."

"Elspeth, that—"

"You don't need to explain," I interrupted. "I get it."

I couldn't meet his gaze and we stood in silence for a moment, our easy banter nowhere to be found.

After a moment, he cleared his throat. "So, you're back?"

I shrugged. "I had two sucky choices. I chose the least sucky."

He snorted.

I bit back as much anger as I could. "It was either run my entire life, constantly look over my shoulder

and endangering everyone I came into contact with…
or come back here and start a war. At least this way I
have a chance of ending it once and for all. And if I
don't, well…*peace be with us.*"

"The prophecy," he murmured.

"*Screw destiny.*" A flash of white-hot anger pulled at
my Colours and…what would I call it? Darkness,
shadows, greyscale, black goop? I could hardly keep
calling it 'the dark thing inside me'.

Rory's gaze finally caught mine. "What
happened?"

I curled my trembling hands into the ends of my
sleeves.

"I was staying on a farm near the northern edge
of Loch Lomond," I told him. "The owners let me
stay in their holiday rental in exchange for working
around the property. I…" I debated telling him about
Dad's journal, but I decided to hold those memories
to myself for now. My mother's face was a blur, but
she was still mine. "I made a mistake and the
Chimera found me. I…" I took a deep breath, my
guilt tugging at the edges of my darkness, "I was with
their young daughter, Florence. She's seven years old
and he held a knife to her throat."

I heard her scream, the sound echoing in my
memory like a nightmare, and I remembered the
terror in her eyes. A monster attacked and I'd killed
it in front of her. Afterwards, she'd thrown herself
into my arms with such blind trust, as if I would
keep her safe always. She'd seen me turn into a

different kind of beast and she still looked to me for protection.

Rory's hands found my face. "Elspeth, *stop*."

I blinked, realising I'd allowed threads of darkness to crawl across my skin. Shaking my head, I knocked his hands away. "I'm sorry, I—"

"What happened next?"

"I killed it," I snapped. "Then another one came after me, wearing the face of her father. I couldn't be responsible for the death of a little girl."

"But you saved her," he argued. "She's fine."

"If it wasn't Florence, then it would be someone else. Maybe not today, maybe not next week, but it would happen eventually."

"So, you've chosen to face them."

I scowled. "Isn't it the heroic thing to do?"

"It's not about heroics. No path in this is easy."

"Of course, it isn't. I bring death wherever I go." The moment I said it out loud, it hit me like a tonne of bricks. Death would follow no matter what I did or where I went. People would die either at my hand or the Chimera's. It was who I was.

Rory's expression faded and he reached for me. "Elspeth—"

"I'm tired," I murmured, jerking away and picking up my bags. "I can't right now."

Not wanting to hear his platitudes, I phased out of the library and landed in my room. No doubt he'd find my new trick annoying, but I didn't care.

Dropping my bags as the crystal light flickered on

overhead, I caught sight of my nwyfre stele. It was still stuck in the wall where I'd stabbed it the day I'd fled the Warren, imbedded an inch deep into the hard turquoise and obsidian.

My fear still controlled me, but I couldn't help it. My choices affected everyone. There was no escape.

I missed the shy, awkward Elspeth I was before. I wanted to go back. I wanted to look in the mirror and see my long, auburn hair and freckly skin. I didn't care if I was isolated and depressed, sitting in my house in western Sydney mourning my dad with no one to help me shoulder the burden. I wanted to be alone. I wanted to be small.

After the last four months, being a nobody didn't seem so bad after all.

6

———

Ignis was asleep at the end of the bed, curled into a tight ball when I woke the next morning. He'd forgiven me for the multiple phases, returning to warm my feet sometime during the night.

I was glad to have my things back and a safe place to rest. A few extra changes of clothes never went astray, though I hadn't brought myself to free my stele from the wall. In a fiery burst of rebellion, I'd hung my scarf and beanie off it.

Hunger finally forced me out of my room.

The Warren was quiet, and the tunnels were eerily silent. I wondered if news of my return had spread and there was a town meeting I hadn't been invited to. I almost turned back, but my stomach gargled in protest at my spinelessness.

One thing I hadn't counted on was how the Druids would react to my return. Delilah had left the door open, but what about everyone else? I had no idea. I hadn't even thought about it, which made me cringe at my self-centredness. It wasn't *just* about me, was it?

The same hesitation I'd felt on my first day in the Warren had come back in a rush as I stood in the doorway of the kitchen. Like the first day of school—or the day after being discovered to be a new supernatural creature—I felt like an oddity underneath a magnifying glass…and they hadn't even noticed me yet.

Druids sat at the stone tables, talking amongst themselves as they ate breakfast. They weren't as animated as they usually were, but after their near miss with the Chimera, I couldn't blame them. Things were volatile right now.

My stomach rumbled and I gazed longingly at the food at the opposite end of the room, but I couldn't seem to make myself move towards it.

I rubbed my arms, soothing phantom prism burns. Was I sweating? I felt like I was standing in an icebox and a sauna at the same time.

"Elspeth?"

A presence at my back caused me to go numb.

The Druid stepped around me, catching my gaze. "Elspeth?"

Darby was looking up at me with an alien mix of concern and shock. Her hair seemed shorter and her tattooed runes brighter.

Upon hearing my name, everyone turned. Silence fell in the kitchens as they stared, stunned. I bet they thought they were done with me and I was never coming back.

I rubbed my arms again and thought about running. Darby was the last person I wanted to see, let alone talk to, right now.

Well, that was a lie. Vanora was right up there with her.

The Druidess cleared her throat. "Listen, I'm—"

"I just came to get something to eat before the Elders call me," I interrupted, forcing my gaze away from hers. "But, I—"

"Let me get something for you," she blurted before I could back away. "Come. Have a seat." She swept her arm out and some of the other Druids rose, offering their spots to me. "Arnold has been making this amazing vegetarian omelet. Would you like to try it?"

I looked around the room. "I don't understand."

Darby frowned and stepped in front of me. "You saved us from the Chimera," she murmured, "even after we were so cruel to you." She cleared her throat. "After *I* was so cruel to you."

Just because I'd saved the Warren, didn't mean I forgave her. She'd been seconds away from stabbing me through the heart before Delilah had stopped her. I could still see the hatred in her eyes and feel the venom of her words, even as the prisms burned their memory across my skin.

"You're part Fae, but you're also a Druid," she

went on. "I let my prejudice towards the Chimera get the better of me."

"I'm not a Chimera," I hissed. "I didn't even know about any of this. I—"

"I know. I…" She pursed her lips together then reached for my hand, but I snatched it away.

"*Don't.*"

Darby recoiled as if I'd slapped her. "Elspeth, I'm sorry. What can I do? Name your price. I'll do anything, just *please forgive me.*"

I couldn't look at the Druids watching us in the kitchens. I couldn't look at Darby, either.

Swallowing my anxiety, I turned and strode away, fleeing through the Warren. I kept my head down, hiding behind a curtain of emerald hair.

After a few turns, I realised I was in the main cavern. *Salle*, the great willow tree, shimmered in ethereal light, her branches fluttering in the simulated breeze. I could feel the complex pattern of prisms keeping her alive, the Colour warm and inviting.

My breathing calmed and my anxiety began to fade.

For all their faults and struggles, the Druids did have Earth's best interests at heart. *Salle* was proof of that.

Sighing, I looked up at the willow and remembered Rory's first lesson on emotional blockage. I'd gone from not feeling enough, to feeling everything I'd bottled up all at once. At least I wasn't going to explode into Colour crystals any time soon. There was that, I supposed.

I had told him that I was a complete reject growing up. I was picked on, bullied, squashed down. I learned to make myself small and quiet to avoid being a target. No one would notice me if I didn't excel, and then I'd be safe.

Fast forward to today, I was different, even amongst the supernatural. I'd gone from nothing to everything all at once. The prophecy, my Fae blood, the dark power simmering just below my Colour, being hunted by the Chimera, almost getting Florence killed… It all had fostered a different kind of loneliness.

I knew I was wallowing in self-pity, but it felt good to be self-destructive without literally exploding for a change.

Approaching the willow, I pressed my palm against the snarled trunk.

You saved us from the Chimera, even after we were so cruel to you.

I tried to push past the memory of what had happened here, but it was still a part of me and would probably linger at the surface for a long time to come.

Deep down, I knew I couldn't keep living the same way I did when I believed I was human. I couldn't be timid, unsure, or second-guess myself. For reasons beyond my control, and for better or worse, I was important. I was born into something bigger than myself. My choices came with a heavy price and that's just the way it was.

But…

What was I supposed to do next? How was I meant to fight back? How could I forgive myself if I couldn't even forgive Darby and Vanora? *How could I honour my father?*

Maybe the Elders would give me direction… because I sorely needed one.

———

It was Ignis who came when the Elders summoned me to the library.

He circled my legs, meowing and pawing at me to get my attention. It took a moment to realise he wanted me to follow—I'd thought he'd wanted to be fed.

Shor Elinian and Rowen Ariennir were seated at the large, oak table at the end of the room. They were waving their hands at one another in a heated, and animated, argument. Strands of Rowen's brilliant burnt orange hair had escaped its neat braid and Shor's usual black shirt had become untucked.

I caught a few words—*darkness, death, battle, and extinction*—before Delilah, who was sitting to one side, coughed, forcing them to fall silent.

The turned, bowing their heads in greeting.

"Come, be seated, Elspeth," Rowen said, her tone

kind and not at all unpleasant. "We have much to discuss."

"I thought…" I glanced between them. "You're not angry with me?"

Shor grunted. "Frustrated is a more apt word in this situation. You ran away without a word, causing chaos all over Scotland."

"I thought I was doing the right thing," I argued. "I—"

"Elspeth," Delilah urged.

I bit my bottom lip and planted my backside in the nearest chair.

"Edinburgh isn't the same place you left behind," Delilah told me in her Elder voice. I wasn't talking to my grandmother like I had been yesterday; no, now it was all business.

"The Chimera are returning," Shor said. "They followed your signature and have resumed their search for the Warren."

"Nothing has changed," Rowen stated. "We're back at the beginning once more."

"They will not find the Warren," Delilah said. "They no longer have the power."

"No longer?" I asked. "What does that mean?"

"The Warren's portals were always active, but dormant," she explained. "They found a way to trace them."

"That's how they…" I remembered the day they attacked while I was working in the kitchens. It was also the day Darby and Vanora had led a mob against me and— yeah, I wasn't going there again.

"You can come and go as you please," Shor said, clearly annoyed, "your abilities allow it. However, the Druids have stricter rites of passage."

"We have decided to retreat into the Warren," Delilah added. "Close the portals and maintain a strict code of passage. No one is to travel to the surface unless it is strictly necessary."

"There aren't any Druids patrolling the city?" I asked.

"Only a select few with the experience to maintain their cover," Shor replied. Likely he was referring to Rory, Jaimie, and Vanora. I hadn't met any of the other Druids who patrolled.

"But it has come with some drawbacks," Delilah said, hinting at the mysterious changes that had emerged since I'd been away.

"Like?"

"Our absence has allowed more creatures to thrive," Rowen told me. "They seem to have taken our retreat as a sign that they can move into our territory."

I blinked. "Fae?"

She nodded.

"I don't understand," I said. "I thought most of the Fae were confined to Ireland."

"We believed so," Delilah said. "But we never knew much about them to begin with."

"The Witches' portals seem to give them more

power to venture farther across the world than we had anticipated," Rowen said, voicing her theory. "Regardless of how powerful they seem to be."

"So, it's not just the Chimera anymore," I murmured. Not all Fae were evil, though. Like humanity, there were good and bad. Who else was out there? "We need to reestablish a presence in the city."

"Easier said than done," Shor stated. Clearly, they already had discussed this point at length.

"We don't know how many there are or where they come from," Rowen added. "After two decades, we're still no closer to finding out their secrets."

Shor turned to me. "We don't have the numbers, but if Elspeth can harness her abilities—"

"We went over this once before," I interrupted. "I won't be the weapon you wield."

"If you want to live amongst the Druids, you must follow our laws," he snapped. "You cannot have it both ways."

I felt a twist of anger drag at the darkness. While the Chimera were multiplying like rabbits, we were down here arguing about who oversaw what.

I took a deep breath, silencing the unstable ability, clearing my head enough to realise Shor had a point. I wasn't in a position of authority and couldn't just do what I wanted without repercussions. There were laws and a hierarchy of leadership for a reason. It was time to be humble and not rush out and try to fix everything myself. Stabbing in the dark was getting me nowhere.

I lowered my gaze and nodded. "What would you have me do?"

Rowen scraped her chair back, rose, and walked around the table. She sat beside me and her stern expression was replaced with something closer to understanding.

"You are in a difficult situation," she said. "We all are. The Druids aren't warriors, Elspeth. The younger generations are doing their best, but we're not as strong as the Chimera. They will beat us time and time again, but with you by our side, we may have a chance at matching them."

"I don't know how to fight," I told her. "Everything I've done so far has been a shot in the dark. I've been making it up. Faking it."

"*Improvising*," she said.

I shook my head. "I can't keep doing it like that. We're talking life and death here."

"That's why we want you to pick up from where you left off," Delilah said. "Continue to learn, to test your boundaries."

"And to do it in the Warren where you are protected," Shor added. "The Chimera will not find us again, though they will try their hardest."

"And we will learn as well," Rowen said. "War is not in our vocabulary, but regardless, war is upon us. Now is the time to prepare, to learn about the Fae and who the Chimera really are…and to learn about ourselves."

"We must unite, Elspeth," Shor stated, his grumpy

exterior turning wise. "We must be clear about our intentions and what we fight for. You may be half-Fae, but you are also an Odhweine. We will not force you to be our sword, but you must decide if our cause is also your own."

"And what do you stand for?"

"Peace," Rowen said. "Maintaining the fragile balance of nature and the nurturing of life. This is the Druid's true calling."

"The threads that bind us are the most mysterious of all," Delilah murmured. "We weave those threads in hope that we may bring nature into harmony with the peoples of the Earth."

Rowen nodded. "All are together, and no one is above."

"We may not have made it through the Darklands," Shor said, "but we still uphold the values we came to this world with. We know no other path."

Thríbhís Mhór. The three spiralled triskele of earth, sea, and sky.

Thinking about the truth I'd dragged from Owen's mind, I knew I'd always choose the Druids. They had their faults and were learning to overcome them, but the Chimera...? Their endgame was crystal-clear.

"You're right," I said. "I ran away. I believed it was the right thing to do in order to protect you all, but I learned a hard lesson. Until the Chimera are gone, there will be no peace in this world." I looked at

Rowen. "They will beat us time and time again… prophecy be damned."

"I agree," she said. "We cannot live by prophecy. We can only follow our conscious."

"So, I continue to learn," I continued. "And my *neach-gleidhidh*?"

The Elders fell silent.

My heart twisted. "Rory doesn't want to be my guardian anymore?"

"We think it is pertinent in this situation to gather wisdom from all Druids," Shor replied. "Each Druid has a strength you will learn from."

I swallowed my disappointment, knowing I had a hand in it. *If only I had phased into my room…*

If the power I wielded was death, then I would command it. Death was a part of life and I would be a guardian of the world between—*a soul who bridged the gap.*

"Then," I said, "shall we begin?"

7

———

The training room was empty.

I stood inside the door, scratching my head. For a bunch of Druids who'd just declared they were going to war, they weren't quick on the uptake.

There was only the bare minimum of equipment —a set of dumbbells, a punching bag with gloves, rolled up yoga mats, and a few other bits and pieces— but it didn't really matter what was in here. I didn't know how to use any of it.

Part of me wanted to find Rory, but the bit of me that was still embarrassed kept me from seeking him out. He was keeping his distance and I was avoiding him, which made for the ultimate invisibility cloak. I hadn't laid eyes on him or caught his scent since we argued in the library.

It wasn't like I had feelings for him. His closeness with Vanora was just a painful reminder of my isolation. I was a unique and unpredictable creature with a target on my back—and getting too close was a bad idea, but it didn't mean I didn't want to feel that closeness with somebody. I just didn't think I was destined for it.

"Elspeth?"

I turned to find Darby behind me, and I bristled. *Please don't tell me the Elders asked her to train me. I'd rather figure it out on my own.*

She crossed the room, stood before me, and said, "Hit me."

I stared at her. "Excuse me?"

"I know you can. You broke my nose, remember? I deserve it. This time I'll let it heal the old-fashioned way."

I screwed up my face.

"C'mon," she declared, gesturing at me. "Aim between the eyes."

"I'm not going to hit you."

"Are you sure?"

"*Yes.*"

She smiled and her body relaxed. "That says a great deal about the kind of person you are," she told me. "If I was in your place, I would have already put you on the floor."

"What is this about?" I asked. "Are you that desperate for my forgiveness?"

She lowered her gaze. "What I did to you was inexcusable. I was so clouded by fear and hatred, I tried to kill you. I *am* trying to make amends here,

Elspeth. We're about to go to war with the Chimera and I don't know what else to do."

I looked her over, taking in her pixie cut and tattooed runes. Forgiveness was hard, but I had to give her the chance. It was the right thing to do, wasn't it? Taking the moral high road or whatever it was called.

"I'm not going to hit you," I said. "So, try something else."

Darby's gaze flew up. "Really?"

"Or I can hit you…if that's what you really want."

"No, I-I want to help you work on your fitness," she said with an air of excitement. "We can put together a program to build up your strength and endurance. It's my skill, you see. Do you like yoga?"

I glanced at the mats rolled up in the corner and realised they were her pet project…and she was one of my assigned—or voluntary, I wasn't sure yet— guardians. The Darkland Druid Elders struck again.

"I don't know anything about yoga," I admitted. "I was an academic kind of person before all of this. Anything fitness-related wasn't my strong suit." I snorted. "I've done more running in the last four months than I had in my entire life."

Darby grinned. "We can start with some basic weight training, then move onto general fitness. I can work out an entire routine for you. Soon, you'll be able to run all the way to the top of Arthur's Seat."

"I doubt it," I shrugged, "but you're the *neach-gleidhidh* in this situation."

She practically skipped over to the line of dumbbells leaning against the wall. "Dumbbells are all about the motion. The way you lift and move them works different muscle groups. Let me show you." She picked up a set of the smaller weights and moved through a range of exercises. "See how my muscles flex when I do this? The more repetitions you do, the more muscle you build. Strength is gained by use and resistance." She offered me the dumbbells. "Now you try."

I glanced at them warily.

"They're not going to bite," she said. "Promise."

"Okay then." I took the weights.

Darby sat me on the bench opposite the mirror. "Follow your movements in the mirror. It'll help you see if you're following the correct motion."

I worked through a few repetitions and it didn't take long for my arms to ache. They were like two wobbly, wet noodles. I had my work cut out for me.

I glanced at the Druidess in the mirror as she fussed with the yoga mats. I was in for some flexibility training after this, I could read it all over her face.

For whatever reason, I recalled the day in the kitchen when Darby had taunted me. Fighting her in that moment had been thrilling and had filled me with a power I'd sorely lacked, even though I knew it wasn't the best way to handle things.

Every Druid has a true name, she'd said. *Whoever knows it has power over your spirit.*

"Darby?" I set down the dumbbells. "When you…

The day we fought in the kitchens, you mentioned something about a true name?"

She tensed, recalling the exact moment she'd threatened me. Sitting beside me, she ran her fingernails underneath one another—a nervous tick.

"True names are linked to our souls," she explained. "Every Druid has one, even you."

"Even me?" I thought about it for a moment. "Why haven't I heard anyone talk about them before?"

"We don't speak of them," she replied. "If someone knows your true name, they can use it against you."

"Use it, how?"

"To bind, to cause pain, and to control." So that's what she meant with she said power over one's spirit.

I frowned. "Do you know yours?"

"No." Darby shook her head. "Nor do I want to. If we were in the homeland, we would be safe to reveal them, but outside of Thríbhís Mhór, they're dangerous. Once your true name is revealed…"

She didn't have to say it. If an enemy knew a Druid's true name, then it was nothing but a miserable life to follow.

"Do the Chimera know about this?" I asked. "It seems dangerous."

"No, they don't. We rarely speak of it as it is and as far as I know, only the older Druids know their true names. They banned the ritual centuries ago for our own protection."

"Oh." I glanced at her tattooed arms. "And those?"

"They connect me with my Colours on a physical level," she explained. "Each rune symbolises an intent, though these are woven with delicate prisms. See?" She waved her hand over a marking on her left forearm and the lines shimmered in a holographic glitter of blues, purples, and greens. "This one helps with my breathing. And this one my balance. That one sharpens my hearing. You have to remember they drain your energy when they're used. Too much and you can find yourself in trouble real fast."

So, they enhanced her abilities with laser focus… with limitations, of course.

"It's also a symbol of dedication to mark oneself," she went on. "It's extreme and not many Druids have them, but they can be useful when we have a certain calling we wish to dedicate ourselves to."

I studied the shapes, taking in the angled lines and gentle curves. Some looked like Norse sigils, others Pagan glyphs, and there were a few that reminded me of geometric Hindu mandalas. She even had tiny symbols on each of her fingers. What I found most interesting was even though they were so different, they wove into each other like a seamless artistic pattern.

"How do you make them?" I wondered out loud.

"With our steles. They're not a tattoo with ink. It's all Colour."

"Magic," I murmured with a smile.

The more we talked, the more I realised I kind of liked her. A part of me wanted to loathe the Druidess for eternity, which made the revelation sting a little.

"So," Darby began, "the night you fought the Chimera, Rory said you used your Fae abilities."

I nodded.

She hesitated, but seemed to gather enough courage to ask, "What do they do exactly?"

"I barely understand it," I replied. "I can teleport. I like to call it phasing. Sounds cooler. I can turn shadows into liquid and summon it other places, like out of the ground..." An image of the stuff dripping from my fingers flashed in my mind. "I don't really know what to call it."

"I wonder what it is?" Darby mused.

I didn't think it was wise to tell anyone about the voices or the dark presence I felt I was channelling. There was too much that made my position here unstable, not to mention that I'd shrugged to reign in the desire to kill when I let the darkness in.

"I always thought it might be negative energy," I said. "Like the dark matter that holds the universe together."

Darby pondered this for a moment. "Interesting. You may be right."

"I think I'm going to have to Google it."

"Good luck trying to connect to the Warren's WiFi," she said with a giggle.

I blinked. "Wait... There's Wifi?"

She shook her head. "No, but we have internet in the safe houses."

Which they couldn't use because I'd lured the Chimera back to Edinburgh, but that wasn't even the half of it. I'd been making trouble for them from the day I was born.

"I am sorry, you know."

Darby seemed genuinely shocked. "Whatever for?"

"It's my fault the Chimera are hunting you in the first place. When I came here, I didn't know about any of this. I was just looking for my family."

"You can't help how or why you were born, Elspeth." She paused then sighed. "It's taken me a long time to come to that conclusion. I believed all Fae were evil like the Chimera. I didn't want to see that I was wrong."

"They killed people you loved and took your freedom. Hate is to be expected."

"Hate is a strong emotion." She sighed once more, showing how tired she was. "Too strong. Perhaps that's why we were destined to remain as shadows in the Darklands."

"That would be saying you're irredeemable," I argued. "I don't believe it's that black and white." I hesitated, not sure if she or the other Druids knew about the pact Merlin had made with the Old Ones. The only reason I knew was courtesy of my father's journal.

Darby looked at me with big, hopeful, eyes. "You think I'm redeemable?"

"I'm sitting here with you while you try, aren't I?"

"True." She clapped her hands together. "Now, let's make that fitness program, huh?"

Later that afternoon, I dragged myself through the tunnels, exhausted and hurting from round one of Darby's 'beginner fitness program'. She swore she wasn't exacting anything malicious on me— apparently, if it hurt, it was working. *Until I tore a muscle.*

The kitchen was calling through the rumbles in my stomach, and I decided to face my anxiety with the Druids head-on.

I turned the corner, following the signs that pointed towards the food, and came to an abrupt halt.

Vanora was walking towards me, her boots thumping against the ground with purposeful steps. My heart flipped and my head screamed for me to run the moment our gazes met—fight or flight was activated.

It was the first time I'd seen her since I'd accidentally phased in on her kissing Rory. All I could think about was how beautiful she was with her raven-coloured locks and angular features…and how perfect they looked together.

The Druidess stopped in front of me. I stared at

her, knowing I looked like a deer caught in the headlights of an oncoming semi-trailer. The question remained—would it run me over and splatter my guts all over the tunnel, or swerve in an attempt to miss a near-fatal collision?

"I—" Vanora pursed her lips together. She was having a difficult time getting her thoughts together, which seemed like a little victory on my behalf. "I wanted to say... I wanted..." She coughed. *"I'm sorry,"* she finally managed to choke out.

"Well, I can see how difficult that was for you," I retorted, unable to help myself.

"Elspeth, *for goodness sake*." Vanora scowled and crossed her arms over her chest. "I did the wrong thing. I didn't give you a chance to prove yourself."

"And was killing a bunch of Chimera enough?"

She snorted.

"I didn't like doing it, you know."

"I don't like killing either, but sometimes you need to protect yourself."

Yourself. That was a telling word. I resisted the urge to add another frustrated snort into the mix.

"It was an accident," I said. "The other night when—"

"I gathered." Was it my imagination, or did Vanora just blush?

My stomach gurgled. "I—"

"I wanted to talk to you about Rory."

I wanted to puke. "You're great together. Congratulations."

"No. I…" This was getting awkward. "Did he tell you about his portals?"

"He mentioned something about working on perfecting them," I replied.

Vanora sniffed and flicked her hair behind her shoulder. "Well, he's…" she sighed and rolled her eyes, "getting a little obsessive about it."

I frowned. "Obsessive?"

"Staying up all night, scribbling in his notebook, pouting. You know. *Obsessive*."

I looked her over. "You're worried about him." It wasn't a question.

"Rory can be rebellious and rash, but deep down, he's the responsible sort. He does things with the best intentions, but…" She shrugged. "This feels different and he won't talk to me about it."

"Why do you want me to talk to him?" I asked. "We barely know each other."

"I have no idea why, but he listens to what you say," she said, her jaw tight. "Maybe if *you* say something, he'll listen. He was your *neach-gleidhidh*. The position comes with certain…*truths*."

I faltered for a moment, wondering if I was imagining things. Was Vanora jealous of me? No, that was the craziest thing I'd ever heard, and I'd heard some pretty crazy things in the last few months.

"I don't know if it's my place," I began. "I mean, I'm not a full Druid."

"Ach, *dùin do ghob*," she declared, her accent thickening.

I raised my eyebrows. She'd just told me to shut my mouth. "You do realise I understand Gaelic, right? It's about the only useful side effect granted to me by my mouldy hair."

Vanora let out a sharp sigh. "Of course, you do."

It seemed admitting she needed help wasn't one of her strong suits, and apparently, asking me for help was like driving a hot poker into her chest. We might never be friends, but we could at least try to get along for the sake of the Warren.

I nodded. "If I see him, I'll give it a try."

Vanora opened her mouth, then shut it with a snap. Finally, she grunted, then strode away.

Looking after her, I pressed my palm over my rumbling stomach.

What a day.

8

During the following two days, I was run ragged by the Druids.

Darby was on my case about sticking to my fitness routine, Delilah was teaching me runes and prisms, Jaimie saw me when he could, and Arnold, the chef, insisted I listened to his history lessons. It seemed time didn't move the same way for Druids as it did for humans. He spoke about historical battles like they'd happened last week, not hundreds of years ago.

Even Vanora had frostily taken me through the first steps of fighting with the long-barbed knives she favoured on patrols. The one Rory had given me was similar, though less spiky and vicious.

And, to her utter exasperation, I still hadn't sought out Rory to talk to him about his portal obsession.

Truthfully, I had no idea what to say to him, let alone how I was going to look him in the eye. When I thought about him, instead of all the help he'd given me, all I saw was him kissing Vanora.

My fist collided with the punching bag with a smack; the blow jarred up my arm and the swear word echoed through the empty training room.

Cursing, I shook out my bandaged hand, wishing the only pair of gloves fit me. The wraps did soften the whacks to my knuckles but gave me a true-to-life experience. The Chimera wouldn't wait for me to put my gloves on before a fight. I had to be able to fight without the aid of Colour or a protective layer.

As Vanora had snootily told me, we couldn't rely solely on supernatural abilities. There might come a day when we were cut off from them and we had to be prepared.

I smacked the punching bag again, letting out another curse—this one was worse than the last and didn't bear repeating.

Ignis had followed me yet again, this time using the yoga mats as his throne. He watched me with an air of amusement that was unnatural for a cat and I shot him an annoyed look.

"I'd like to see you try," I told him. "You don't even have opposable thumbs."

"Like to see who try what?" A familiar voice boomed across the training room and I turned to see the impossibly bulky, *and hairy*, Jaimie Frasier grinning at me.

I liked to think the black mop of hair on his head and chest was a side effect of his status as a shapeshifting Druid—he favoured turning into a large, black German Shepard—but it was impossible to tell. Either way, he was like the fun older brother I'd never had.

"Jaimie!" I leapt across the room and threw my arms around his neck.

He returned my embrace, holding me tight against his muscled chest. "Ach, not quite the greeting I was expecting."

"I've been avoiding everyone since I got back," I told him a little sheepishly. "I'm sorry I didn't come find you."

"Understandable," he replied. "I've been up in the city anyway."

My ears pricked. "The city? What's going on up there?"

He shrugged. "Same old, same old. The Chimera are returning. There's a new leader, but so far, we haven't been able to identify who they are." My shoulders sank and the Druid leaned down so he could look me in the eye. "Don't fash, Elspeth. They would have come back if you were here or not. You bought us time we sorely needed."

"I totally screwed you, no matter what choice I made. It's a bitter pill to swallow."

"Ach." He ran his hand through his wild black hair. "I know you think you're a failure, lass, but you're doing the best you can. We all are."

"Who've you been talking to?" I grumbled. "Rory is such a—"

"Your face says a thousand words," he retorted before I could say something I'd regret. "As does your right hook." Jaimie noticed Ignis on the yoga mats and chuckled. "He's following you more and more… And he turned into a tiger to fight with you. That's a shape even I can't master."

"He showed up right before I came back, after I used my…" I coughed.

"Your freaky black goop?"

"Yeah." I laughed, I couldn't help it. 'Freaky black goop' was a pretty accurate description. "Are you my *Fight Club* guardian?"

He chuckled. "I suppose I am."

"So, what am I doing wrong? My whole arm hurts like hell."

"You've got spaghetti arms," he told me, grabbing my elbow and giving it a wobble. "When you punch, your strength comes from your whole body. Use your upper body and shoulder to propel your fist, and don't twist your waist. When you land a blow, it won't jar your arm." He shouldered the bag, steadying it with his bulk. "Give it another go."

I punched again, following his directions. My fist slammed against the bag and this time, it hurt less.

"Good," Jaimie said. "Keep going and try your left, too. It pays to practice with your less dominant side."

I went through a few repetitions, alternating from left to right. After a moment, I stepped back. "Jaimie?"

He peeked around the bag. "Hmm?"

"What's it like? Changing, I mean."

"It feels like throwing up while every bone in your body breaks." He winked and nudged the bag with his fist. "I'm used to it now, but the first few times it made me sick as a dog."

"I hope that pun was intended."

He chuckled. "Of course."

"And your parents? Could they shapeshift, too?"

"My ma could," he replied. "My da doesn't have a special skill. Not many Druids can do what we do."

I bit my bottom lip. He spoke of his mother in the past tense, though his father still seemed to be here.

"A lot of us are orphans, Elspeth," he said, spotting the deepening flush on my cheeks. "Don't fash yourself about it. You're not to blame, lass. Life has never been easy for the Darkland Druids."

"I know, I guess…" I shrugged. "It doesn't make it hurt any less."

"The past is done." Jaimie nudged my shoulder with his fist. "Now is the time to learn how to fight the Chimera."

I grimaced. "By smacking around a punching bag?"

Jaimie nodded. "Next time, the bag might be an ugly grey face with sharp teeth. Best know how to kick a couple of those pointers out, eh, lass?"

I shuffled back to my room at the end of another long day, my mind stuffed full of prisms, yoga poses, and all the ways I could sever major arteries.

Ignis was asleep on the bed when I walked in. Shaking my head, I sat beside him, my muscles aching. If there was a rune for soothing abused tendons, no one had the foresight to teach me.

Flexing my fingers, I wondered what Dad would say if he could see me now.

That's when a spark ignited in my brain. *I could Spirit Walk…*

Going back into death wasn't something I was all that keen to do when I was outside the Warren. The chill of the greying world was eerie at best, and the colourless form Dad had taken was strange. It was him, but it wasn't…at least, not in the way I remembered.

Now I was back in a place where I was protected from the Chimera, temptation to try again was growing. I was supposed to be working on strengthening my abilities and learning what it meant to be a Druid so I could be the best warrior I could in the war to come. Spirit Walking was part of that. At least, I could use it to my advantage, right?

Sighing, I looked at my bag. Should I get out Dad's journal again? I remembered seeing some runes in there that he'd used for protection. Portals were dangerous to the untrained and could blow back a burst of energy, not to mention all the things that could come out of them from other places. Maybe it was the same with the spirit world?

I shivered at the thought of a dark spirit latching onto me and crawling back into life like some kind of leech. *Gross.*

Maybe I should wait and ask Delilah. Or maybe I should grow a pair and take a chance.

But this is actual death we're talking about, Elspeth, I thought. *It's not like taking a plane to the other side of the world for a holiday.*

Shut up, I told my wandering thoughts. Spirit Walking seemed like a walk in the park compared to the negative energy—otherwise known as the black goop—I summoned.

I leapt off the bed, disturbing Ignis, who lifted his head, and grabbed the journal out of my bag. Flipping through it, I found the page where Dad had scrawled the series of runes he'd used to surround his portal experiments.

I thought of Rory, wondering if he used the same kind of precautions. *Damn it. I'd have to confront him after all.*

With a sigh, I wrenched my stele out of the wall and inspected the blade. It was still sharp, the stone hadn't dulled or chipped the edge at all. The quartz crystal on the end glinted in the light as I turned it over. I hadn't really used it before, but it couldn't be that hard, right?

I wondered if I'd need blood to seal my intent or

if I was determined enough not to have to cut myself to get this done.

Following the directions in the journal, I marked the runes on the floor. The stele moved back and forth, forming glowing lines as I worked around the circle—no blood needed. Thankfully, the knife didn't gouge holes into the actual floor since all the runes were temporary. They hovered slightly above the turquoise and obsidian stone like delicate holograms, glittering and buffeting slightly as I moved around them. *Beautiful.*

Ignis watched from his perch on the bed. His eyes were sharp and his tail swished back and forth. I was glad he was here, though I could sense the disapproval in his glare.

When I was done, I stood in the centre of the circle and pocketed my stele.

This time we'd have time to speak. I could ask all the questions I was dying to know the answers to—*pun unintended.*

"Okay," I said to myself more than to Ignis. "Time to be reckless. Death is my middle name."

White mist crept under the door, stretching into the room with long spectral fingers. Warmth and colour bleached out of the world and death reached for me.

The veil passed over me and I stepped forwards, forging a path deeper into the realms of death. I looked back, but like the night I'd first Spirit Walked, I'd left nothing of myself behind. Creepy.

This time it had been easier than ever. Shaking off uneasiness, I turned towards the grey lands governed by the spirits.

To my surprise, Ignis padded next to me, his tabby cat form shedding as he grew into a great muscled tiger. I gaped at him as the prisms of his construct glittered and changed, settling in his glowing stripes. This place was devoid of colour, so seeing this felt like I was in a cinema watching an old black and white movie.

"Excuse me," I declared. "When, where, why, what, *how?*"

Ignis just swished his large tail and licked his whiskers. Yeah right, like I was getting an answer out of him. *Pfft.*

It was weird walking beside a tiger and not be worried it was going to turn around and eat me. Rory was right about him after all. Ignis must have had some serious magic when his soul was intact, otherwise he wouldn't be standing with me in the land of the dead.

"Is this how you travel around?" I asked him. "You use death as a superhighway?" I wouldn't be surprised. I seemed to be connected to this place through the Druids and the Fae.

Ignis sat beside me, his gaze moving to the misty reaches of the void, keeping a silent vigil.

I focused on my father, contouring an image of him in my mind. Then I waited.

And waited.

And waited some more.

After a while, my heart sank. He wasn't here.

I looked around at the swirling mist, the echo of the living world I'd left behind a blur around me. It was then I realised that this wasn't the final stop for the dead. Where I walked was only a weigh-station to the afterlife.

It served the same purpose as the Darklands, but this was a place all souls must navigate at one point or another. I gathered people got stuck, lost, or were rejected entirely. Perhaps this was where Ignis's damaged soul was destined to roam before Delilah caught it.

Upon thinking of the cat, he sat beside me and pressed his giant paw on top of my foot. He grunted, his tiger voice echoing through the mist.

"What is it?" I asked, burying my fingers into his wiry fur.

Of course he didn't reply, he couldn't, but he sat next to me and lent me his courage.

Dad was gone.

He'd crossed over to the afterlife, or the next life after that. I got the feeling whatever happened next wasn't for me to know, not until it was my time to pass.

I sighed and swallowed the lump in my throat. If I'd known the last time I would ever see him was that night in Calton Cemetery, I might have done things differently.

Even then, I'd known it would be like this. His

soul was already fading, content in the knowledge he'd raised a courageous young woman—even though I knew nothing about the supernatural world.

"He had so much faith in me," I said to Ignis. "How could I have so little in myself?"

Ignis lapped at my hand, his barbed feline tongue rasping against my skin.

"I know. Common sense tells me to forget my doubts and go for it." I snorted. "Why is letting go always the hardest part? Things always get easy once you do."

The tiger nudged his head against my leg, then padded away, moving lightly through the mist.

"Ignis?" I called.

He stopped and glanced back at me. He wanted me to follow, so I gathered my courage and did just that.

We didn't go far before he sat and lowered his head. The mist swirled around his feet, and to my astonishment, a human figure peeled away from the tiger construct.

Had he needed to go farther into the spirit world to gather enough energy to shed the prisms of his earthly body? *Seemed like it.*

I held my breath as the figure rose, unfurling to its full height. Ignis was trying to show me who he'd been. *Who he still was.*

Finally, a man stood before me, tall and muscular. He was blurred, but parts of him were sharp and clear. An arm, a hand, a wave of colourless hair, a slice of stubbled cheek, the edge of an eye with long lashes. I couldn't make out much more, but there was enough to get a sense of who he might have been. The sword in his right hand, even blurred, was a dead giveaway.

I didn't know much about this place or what I was supposed to see, but I felt like the blade wasn't a part of him, but a manifestation of his identity.

As I stared him, I knew his soul wasn't broken. It was blurry, like someone had taken an eraser and attempted to buff him out of existence.

We gazed at one another—me looking up at his tall stature, and him attempting to see me through the haze of his patchy soul. Delilah had unknowingly saved him from a fate worse than floating around in limbo for eternity.

"You were a warrior once, weren't you?" I asked. "A warrior from another world."

He nodded, the movement slow and clunky, as if his spirit fought against him. Holding out his hand, he beckoned for me to take it.

I had no reason not to trust him. Ignis had helped me, fought beside me, and even though he was annoying as hell sometimes, he was yet another one of my guardians. My *neach-gleidhidh*.

I took his hand—though I couldn't feel it—and he showed me what he could remember.

A great battle on a hillside. Swords clashing. A crumbled tower carved out of the side of a ragged cliff. A crystal shard with a milky centre. A woman screamed for him to stop, but he knew there were people counting on him—a whole world of them. Then a white light, a farewell, and fading. Then he was in the Warren, battered and confused, but familiar Colour leeched into his world…and then I was there—an elfish, green-haired woman with no clue.

I blinked as the mist calmed around us, wishing I could embrace the man…*Ignis*.

Whatever had happened, he'd sacrificed himself to save others and his soul had paid the ultimate price.

"Oh, Ignis…" I knelt in front of the tiger as the fractured man dissolved back into the construct.

He bumped his head against mine and I rubbed my nose.

I wished he could talk and tell me everything, but we seemed to be able to communicate despite it. He seemed to have retained some of his former self and brought it into his new life.

I smiled and scratched his chin, feeling a little silly treating him like a pet cat after seeing a glimpse of his past life. A bad-arse warrior was now a shape-shifting cat…and he could recall pieces of it. Delilah said the fractured souls she saved were so fragmented they never retained memories, but Ignis could. This changed things.

"Are you mad Delilah put you into her construct?" I asked, gazing into his eyes. "I doubt you expected it, huh?"

Ignis shook his head and purred. I took it as a no.

he didn't mind, and felt at ease. Perhaps helping my tragic arse gave him new purpose.

"Okay, well, I think we ought to go back. Dad isn't here, but we've learned a lot. Experience is understanding, huh?"

I rose and looked back the way we'd come. Ignis walked beside me and together, we returned to life, both of us a little wiser…

And a great deal stronger.

9

____

It took me several days to realise Rory was waiting for me to make the first move.

I had a lot to learn about relating to people after spending my formative years avoiding them at all costs—a lifelong after-effect of bullying, I supposed.

Ignis helped me find him, padding through the Warren like a bloodhound with me on his tail.

I held two leather-bound books in my hands. One was newly acquired and filled with notes Delilah had made me take on prisms. The other was a kind of peace offering—my father's journal with his portal research. There wasn't anything too personal in it, but maybe Rory would find something to help him with what he was struggling with.

Ignis stopped outside a door in the unfamiliar tunnel and looked back at me. I thought I'd seen all the Warren, but the tunnels looked so alike, I guessed it was easy to become turned about and forget which ones I'd explored.

"He's in here?" I asked the cat.

He meowed and circled around my legs, then disappeared. I guessed he didn't want any part of the conversation that was about to follow, even as a silent spectator. Thinking about what he'd shown me in death, I smiled. Perhaps I was selling the cat short—he probably had enough tact *intact* to know this needed to be hashed out in private.

My heart beating wildly, I eased open the door and went inside.

This room was more obsidian than turquoise, so it was a little dark and dingy. It reminded me of a dungeon, and the crystal sconces on the walls only added to the Medieval allure.

I stepped farther into the workshop, wondering if this was where my father had conducted his portal research. A colourful array of Turkish rugs lay on the floor, some adorned with blackened scorch marks. I guess that was a yes, unless Rory was a little less careful with his Colours. Didn't seem like him, though.

Looking around the room, I didn't spot the Druid straight away. Shelves filled with raw gemstones and minerals lined the walls, the points and facets glinting in the light of the prisms which glittered in the sconces.

It was the Druid version of a science lab.

Rory sat at a table covered in crystal shards with a

journal open in front of him. He was scrawling on the pages, oblivious to everything around him, even the time of day. I took in his rumpled clothes and the way his hair stuck up at the side, like he'd fallen asleep where he sat. I doubted he'd shaved in a week by the length of stubble on his chin. Had he been down here since I got back?

Vanora was right to be worried. I'd never seen him like this.

"Rory?"

He raised his head and stared at me like I was an apparition. In some ways, I was, but I wasn't sure if the way he looked at me was due to his lack of sleep or if he was genuinely shocked that I'd come to see him at all.

"Vanora asked me to check in on you," I told him.

"Well, if Vanora asked you, it must be serious," he drawled, turning his attention back to his journal.

"She told me you're up all night, obsessively plotting prisms, not paying attention to her—"

"Is this about Vanora kissing me?" He narrowed his eyes. "Is that why you've been avoiding me?"

I snorted and pinched the bridge of my nose. "*Men.*"

"Elspeth. How many times do I have to tell you? Vanora isn't my girlfriend." She was just his genetic match, who one day he was honour-bound to make a baby with. To ensure the survival of the Druids, of course. It wasn't supposed to be fun. *Yeah, right.*

"This isn't about her," I snapped. "It's about you

and your portals. She's worried you've become obsessive."

"Obsessive?" he spluttered.

"Yes, and I can see why." I looked over his rumpled clothes. "When was the last time you showered?"

"This m—" He snapped his mouth closed and took on a puzzled expression.

I sighed. "You're supposed to be helping me master my Colour."

"You don't need help with that," he declared, dismissing me. He looked at his journal and began scribbling again. "You're like a prodigy or whatever. I showed you how to get started, and you went off and did it all yourself."

"*Rory.*" I slammed my fist down on the tabletop, making the crystals rattle.

He glanced up at me. "What?"

"If you were around, you would have been there to help me Spirit Walk last night."

"You Spirit Walked on your own?" he asked. "With no training?"

"I've done it before. It's no big deal."

"No big—" He threw his hands into the air and scoffed, "It's a huge deal, Elspeth. You could walk into death and never come back. You could get lost on the other side."

It never occurred to me, but that's because it wasn't a problem. I always knew where I was, almost like I had an anchor that led me home. I wondered if it was tied to my phasing.

"Are you even listening to me?" Rory demanded.

I shrugged. "Only a little."

He rolled his eyes and scoffed, "You're doing that reverse psychology thing humans use, aren't you?"

"So what if I am?" I snapped. "It's the same way you're treating me right now, you arrogant twat."

He shot to his feet. "You're calling me an arrogant twat?"

"I most certainly am!"

"The Darklands are important!" he raged. "So is the homeland! It's our birthright, Elspeth!"

"What good is a portal to nowhere when the Chimera are here right now?" I demanded. "The Darklands are out of reach, Rory. We have to look at the here and now. The Druids and the Warren are what matter. War is on our doorstep, and making a portal to an even worse world with more things waiting to kill us is not a good use of our time."

"Wow," he said, blinking. "Did you take a breath anywhere in the midst of that tirade?"

"It's the truth, not a tirade. One day, when this is all over, maybe then we can look for the Darklands."

"Or I can look for them now so we have a chance to return home if things fall apart," he retorted.

I clenched my fists around the journals in my hands, silently cursing his stubborn streak. "Don't you have any faith in me?" I asked, wanting to smack the books against his stupid face. "You were the one who pleaded with me to go with you. You saved me from the Chimera, Rory. You taught me what it meant to be a Druid. I know I've made mistakes, but I'm trying to help you. You're driving yourself mad looking for a path that's closed to us."

"*It's not closed,*" he snapped.

"Right now, it is." I rounded the table and stood before him. "Rory, you're scaring me."

His eye twitched.

"You were the first person I trusted in a very long time," I admitted. "I told you things I could barely admit to myself, so you know me coming to you like this *means something.*"

"Vanora was the one who threw herself at me," he said. "And you wouldn't let me explain. You turned your back on me."

"I was embarrassed!"

He rolled his eyes.

"I—" I blinked back a sudden flood of tears. "I'm different. I'm not destined for anyone because my blood isn't pure. When I saw you together, I…" I swallowed the lump in my throat. "It was a reminder of all the things I want but will never have." I scoffed and turned away so I could hide. "And now I've made your intervention all about me. I'm the arrogant twat, not you."

Embarrassed beyond belief, I wanted to walk away again to save myself from hearing what he'd say next. I was terrified I'd just ruined the last shreds of my friendship with Rory, that he'd finally realise just how much hard work I was. Maybe that's why I'd always been so isolated—I was just too complicated to deal with.

Knowing and hearing were two different things… and one was worse to take than the other.

The silence seemed to roar in my ears, my sullied blood swishing through my veins like a hurricane, forcing my heart into an unpredictable rhythm.

"You should really stop with the portals," I finally managed to say. "If you won't listen to me, learn from my father's mistakes." I set my dad's journal on top of the table.

"I'm not your father," he stated.

"*Arsehole*." I began to walk across the room, my anger rising to the point where darkness began to hiss around the edges of my vision.

"*Elspeth*."

I forced myself to stop and turn around.

"I'm sorry, okay. I—" He ran his hand over his face.

I held up my hand as the blackness faded from my fingers. "Do you think I want to be like this? Do you think I like to be reminded of how my father screwed you all?"

"*I'm sorry*," he said more firmly. "But this is different."

"It's exactly the same."

Rory's jaw tightened, but he didn't reply. He knew I was right. After all, Dad had the same good intentions.

His brow creased. "Why would you Spirit Walk?"

Sighing, I held my prism journal against my chest. "The night I… The night I…" I couldn't manage to say it. "*You know.*"

Rory was beginning to look concerned that something was fundamentally wrong with me. "Yes, I know."

"I Spirit Walked to get their attention and I spoke to my dad. I know it's stupid, but I hoped he was still around."

"It's not stupid."

I shrugged.

"Did you find him?" Rory asked.

"The spirit world where I went isn't the final stop," I murmured. "I figured that out when he wasn't there."

"I'm sorry."

I shrugged. "I have to come to terms with the fact that he's gone and there's nothing I can do about it. Magic isn't a cure-all."

He snorted. "Still, it was reckless."

"I used some runes for protection," I retorted. "And Ignis went with me."

Rory balked. "The flea bag went into death with you?"

"He's not a flea bag," I grumbled. "He showed me who he was."

"And?" He seemed excited about this and I forgot for a moment how bad the Druid smelled.

"He was a warrior of some kind. I could only see

the parts of him that Delilah managed to save, but he had a sword and I could sense something supernatural. He sacrificed himself to save his world."

"He's in good company then," Rory said.

"I think he knew the price was his soul," I went on, thumbing at the cover of my journal.

"Then that makes him even more special."

"He seems content being inside a construct, but I wish he could tell me…"

"Don't worry about Ignis," Rory told me. "He seems to know enough of his own mind to do as he pleases, and what pleases him is annoying the hell out of you."

I smiled, my heart at ease for the first time since I'd returned. Things seemed to have smoothed between Rory and I, though they were still a little tense. He hadn't made any comment about my admission of romantic loneliness. I couldn't blame him. It was awkward.

"What's in the book?" He poked at the cover.

I looked down at my journal and flipped it open. "Delilah's teaching me Ignis's prisms. All ten thousand of them."

"That's a little bit of an exaggeration, isn't it? There aren't ten thousand of them."

"Okay then. There's nine thousand, nine hundred and ninety-nine." I sighed for what felt like the millionth time that day. I sure wasn't running out of oxygen any time soon. "I feel like I'm running out of time. How can I possibly learn everything I need to before the prophecy comes knocking?"

Silence bloomed between us as our reality weighed heavy on my shoulders.

"You are not death," Rory murmured. "Never say that, okay?"

I looked up at him, surprised he would even bring it up. No matter how true it was, I'd said it to him that day in the library in a moment of exhausted frustration.

"You're forgetting the most important part," he added.

"No, I'm not."

"Yes, you are." He held out his hand and I held my breath as a thread of Colour pooled in his palm. It grew larger, forming lines, corners, and curves, until a sparkling red rose bud burst into life. "You may believe your Fae side is evil, but you also have the power to bring light to dark places. You are a Druid, Elspeth. Never forget that."

I took the rose bud from him and twirled the stem between my fingers. The prism glittered as it spun, reminding me of how magical our world really was. Nothing was perfect, even this, but as Druids, we were blessed.

"Sure," I said, letting the bud dissolve back into Colour. "But you have to promise me one thing."

"Which is?"

"For the love of Colour, take a shower. *You stink.*"

10

It wasn't long before I was summoned by a new instructor—one who was devoted to the Druids deepest and most sacred calling, plants.

I knew where the garden was, but I'd never been inside. Ignis came along, the cat padding silently beside me as we wound our way through the Warren. It seemed the Druids had great success in growing living things in their DIY crystal cave, especially if the food pumped out by the kitchen was anything to go by. But how they did it, was a mystery I hadn't thought to solve on my own.

When I stepped into a long, tall cavern with its own crystal ceiling, I was full of questions…which were quickly forgotten when I beheld the sight before me.

Rows upon rows of plants grew underneath bright, crystal lights. Hot houses had been set up in the back, and I had visions of vines laden with giant juicy tomatoes. I spotted all kinds of flowers, succulents, vegetables, and herbs.

These weren't prisms like the majority of *Salle* or the thousands of little plants growing in cracks and crevices throughout the Warren; these were the real deal. I knew enough about the Druid's affinity with nature to understand that herbs made out of prisms were useless, but ones grown from a seed nurtured by Colour were precious.

I shook my head as I wandered through the garden, stopping to sniff flowers and smell herbs. This place never ceased to amaze me—both in good and bad ways.

Ignis bounded underneath a raised flowerbed, disappearing into the depths of the garden, meagre to do some exploring of his own. Hoping he wouldn't knock anything over, I looked for Osna, the Druidess in charge.

Osna was one of the oldest of the Darkland Druids and knowledgeable about everything green that grew out of the Earth. Apparently, the plants here were not that different from those they'd left behind on the other Earth—they were exactly the same.

I found the Druidess struggling with a bright green plant with long purple flowers as she attempted to transfer it to a new, larger pot.

She was smaller than I'd imagined, tiny in fact. Her shorty, curly, grey hair was tinted blue, her skin was wrinkly with age, and her fingernails were caked with dirt. Paired with her stained trousers and wooly jumper, she looked the part of an outdoors woman. She also seemed to be full of an energy—a spirit, I was envious of.

"Are you Osna?" I enquired.

"Aye." She nodded and waved me forwards. "Help me with this, would you?"

With gnarled hands, she showed me how to grasp the base of the plant as she worked the old pot off the bottom. After a moment, it came loose and dirt sprinkled over the floor.

"What kind of plant is this?" I asked as I carefully set it into its new home. "It looks like lavender, but it doesn't smell like it."

"This is Anise Hyssop," Osna replied, loosening the roots with her bare hands. "Rare, difficult to grow in this part of the world, but extremely useful."

I raised my eyebrows. "Difficult to grow?"

The Druidess chuckled. "Not in here, it isn't. A little crystal light, a touch of Colour, and up she goes."

"So this is where the kitchens gets all its produce," I mused as she dumped fresh soil into the pot to stabilise the plant.

"Plants aren't just for eating," Osna declared. "Come. Oh, and carry that, would you?" She jabbed a finger at the Anise Hyssop we'd just repotted.

I picked up the plant and carried it against my chest, following the Druidess as she weaved through the garden and under a stone arch.

A second cavern lay beyond, though this one was smaller, but no less crammed with greenery.

A large, peculiar tree grew in the centre, the trunk thick and heavy looking, and forked in the middle. The canopy covered the entire ceiling, the branches twisting so thick it reminded me of the wormy curves of a human brain. A layer of spiky green foliage sat at the very top, so thick it looked like a strange hat, though it was mostly hidden by the impressive undercarriage.

"*Dracaena Cinnabari*," Osna said, following my gaze. "Otherwise known as the dragon blood tree. It grows in Yemen."

I blinked. "Yemen?"

"Yes. *Yemen*." Osna sighed. "This one is larger than they grow in their natural habitat. I'm afraid I got a little heavy-handed. They're endangered, you know."

"You're trying to protect it?"

"Of course! I can't save everything, but I try."

"Do you use it for anything?"

"The humans use it for dye and incense," she said with a huff. "And they think it's *magic*."

"Magic?"

"The sap is red. I suppose it looks a little like blood, but dragons?" She huffed again. "It can do a lot of things when paired with the right ingredients, but I doubt they know them. Rare plants from opposite ends of the Earth and all. Look." She tapped the trunk where a tap had been placed. "Unique tree, this. Full of antioxidants. Paired with Anise Hyssop, it can relieve cardiac arrest."

"Really?" I asked, my eyes widening.

"It won't bring back the dead, but if a heart is barely beating or out of rhythm, pop a bit of that in your mouth. It'll fix you right up."

"Plants can do that?" I wondered out loud.

"Of course, they can!" Osna shot me a dirty look that had me sweating. "Put that there." She pointed to an empty spot in the midst of a cluster of other herbs, and I set the heavy pot into place.

How she knew what everything was and where it went was beyond me. There had to be thousands and thousands of different plants here.

"The Elders told me I'm supposed to teach you about herbs," she told me, "though what you need them for is beyond me. I don't like to teach young things about poisons."

"Poisons?"

Osna sighed. "You want to fight the Chimera, yes? Kill them all dead?"

"I want them to stop coming after us," I told her. "Killing them isn't exactly something I want to do, but what other choice have they given us?"

The Druidess clucked her tongue and shoved me towards a table at the far end of the cavern. It was covered in papers, mortar and pestles, scales, and various delicate bottles, leaving hardly any room to move. In other words, organised chaos. I was beginning to suspect it was a theme around here.

"Herbs, roots, resins, and blossoms all have a purpose," she began. "Flowers aren't just for smelling pretty, herbs don't just make your food taste nice, resins aren't just sticky, and roots don't just suck up water into the plant." I listened carefully, wondering if she'd taken a breath at all.

"Yes, I know," I said.

Osna snorted and slapped my hand with a stick. Where she'd materialised that from was beyond me.

"Ow. What was that for!" I exclaimed.

"Listen and learn," the Druidess told me. "Don't presume. Quiet your mouth and be like the root." I stifled a snort. "Absorb the things I tell you like the root absorbs the water. You hear me?"

It didn't take me long to realise her sharp change in character was her 'teacher mode'—a curious remnant from an eighteen-hundreds' schoolhouse—and she took it extremely serious. For the next hour, she walked me though the basics of every common medicinal herbs and flowers in her collection, of which there were *a lot*.

Chamomile, lavender, dandelion, garlic, basil, marigold, peppermint, and St. John's Wort were just the tip of the iceberg. She made me smell *and* taste them all. I quickly learned that not all of them were remotely nice.

When Ignis appeared and began eyeing her collection of bottles and vials, she shooed him away with her stick before he could knock any of them off the table.

Osna was at least a thousand years old, and a little batty, but I quite liked her in an eccentric way. When she wasn't rapping my knuckles, that was.

At the end of the lesson, she fished around in her collection of distilled oils and balms.

"Here," she told me, holding up a vial. "Dragon's Breath."

I glanced at her curiously.

"*Dracaena Cinnabari.* For your heart," she said with a roll of her eyes. "I won't have a hand in killing, even if it is those foul Fae creatures. Plants are for life. *For healing.* I didn't come from the other Earth and survive the Darklands to be an accessory to war. If you get into trouble, this will fix you." She grinned and forced the bottle into my hand. "I added a little something extra. Those Chimera like to poison things, or so I hear. You might need it before long."

"Thank you, Osna, I don't know what to say."

She huffed and shook her head. "You just said it, silly girl."

My heart was lighter when I went to bed that night.

After my morning with Osna, I had another yoga session with Darby. I was still awkward and screwed all the poses up, but I did feel like I was getting stronger. I ached less, that was for sure.

By the time I made it back to my room, I had just enough energy to fall into bed before my eyes closed.

My dreams had been empty ever since Owen had attempted to invade them, and I hadn't thought twice about it. I rarely remembered what I saw when I slept, so it wasn't of much concern. I figured I'd just simply forgotten the next morning.

But tonight I was aware that I wasn't where I was supposed to be.

One moment I was curling up under the blankets, and the next, I was standing in a graveyard in the dark. I recognised the headstones and the church looming out of the gloom. *Greyfriars.*

Was it merely my memory conjuring the place I had first laid eyes onto the Chimera or was it intentional?

It definitely wasn't an accidental phase, it was a dream. I was fully clothed, wearing the same things I'd had on the night I first arrived in Edinburgh—my leather jacket, jeans, knitted jumper, and worn in combat boots.

Looking up, I expected the city to be looming over the kirkyard, casting an orange glow against the overcast sky, but it was dark. My dream hadn't filled in that part, neither had it bothered to give me a sense of the chill in the air.

I turned, mist swirling around the headstones. My feet didn't move like they should—the soles of my boots felt as if they were solid blocks of metal, and I'd stepped into a thick layer of sticky tar along the way.

Whispers echoed at the edges of my hearing. First from the left, then behind, then off into the distance.

The words were indistinguishable, but it didn't stop me from trying to catch one or two, though I wasn't even sure they were in English.

I stood before the statue, gazing up at the weeping angel. Her wings drooped as if she protected the grave below and marble tears dripped down her cheeks. A wreath of flowers and leaves sat atop her head and her arm stretched out, pointing downwards.

I was suddenly reminded of a quote I'd heard at one time or another. *A fool looks at the finger that points to the sky,* and I smirked. I'd probably heard it in a book or movie, though my dream had brought up the memory in order to tell me something.

I looked down and read the words carved into the headstone. *Yenris'del lingers at the World's End.* It was more than a little strange and didn't seem like something just anyone would write on the monument of their life. Yenris'del? What was that?

The hairs on the back of my neck bristled as I felt eyes glare at me somewhere in the shadows of my mind.

I knew the feeling they brought with them. After trying to evade them for three months, I'd grown accustomed to the tingling in my fingertips and learned that it was a warning from the unstable mix of supernatural elements growing inside me.

The Chimera were here.

I didn't think they'd be stupid enough to try, but we were all getting a little desperate, right?

I could try to force myself to wake up or try to

reach Ignis, but maybe— *No,* it was reckless. Indecision flooded my mind, but one thought persisted. *Maybe I could learn something useful.*

It was my dream and I was the one in control here, even though I couldn't figure out how to wake just yet. The Chimera were in my world now.

I reached down to my hip and pulled out my knife, the blade materialising from nothingness. Its weight was comforting in my hand as I dragged my heavy body through the kirkyard.

"I know you're here," I called. "Show yourself! Let's talk, Chimera."

Movement parted the mists and a dark figure appeared. A tall man made himself known, his greying features dim in the shadows, but his true form was unmistakable.

I brandished the knife. "I've declared for the Druids. They are my family, not the Chimera. I will retaliate if you come here again."

The Fae didn't move.

"Do you understand?" I prodded.

The Chimera smiled, showing his row of pointed teeth and said, "*Boo.*"

I screamed as he rushed towards me, his spirit peeling from his body. One word flashed into my mind and my blood ran cold.

Possession.

I woke with a start and Ignis hissed, his eyes big and black as he stared at me. My shoulder stung and I pressed my palm against the tear in my bare skin.

He'd scratched me awake, helped me break free of the dream…for the second time.

"*Ignis*," I said with a gasp. "*Bloody hell.*"

My room brightened as the light eased on, awoken by my loose hold on my Colours.

Satisfied I was still myself, Ignis headbutted me and rubbed his face against my cheek. I wrapped my arms around him and held his furry body close as my heart rattled inside my chest.

My Fae side was calling out for my other people. It was a beacon, like the one that had drawn me to the Darkland Druids—only this time, away from my dreams, it felt as if my blood had turned into white-hot magma.

I gritted my teeth and let the pulse run its course, my brow beading with sweat.

Why hadn't I felt it until now? I swallowed hard as I realised it was because someone was calling out to me. They'd picked up the phone, so to speak, and dialled my number. I could declare for the Druids all I wanted, but it wouldn't change my DNA.

Thanks for the reminder.

"They're really back," I whispered after a moment. It was easy to forget about the world above while living down in the Warren.

Thinking about the presence in my dream, I scowled. It wasn't Owen—he was dead and gone. No, Owen was small-time compared to whoever was on the other end of the line.

"I'm not picking up," I told Ignis. "I'm blocking their number."

I hesitated. Could I do that? I guess I just had to give it a try. There was nothing else for it.

Laying back down, Ignis stretched out beside me, his eyes narrowing as he watched my eyes droop.

"No need to panic," I murmured as I fell back to sleep. "They can't find us here…"

Ignis, on the other hand, kept a silent vigil over me until morning, his claws at the ready.

11

———

In the week that followed, life was settled for the first time since my father had died.

Things had become easier between Rory and I, my training was progressing, and I felt more in tune with my new reality. There were still many unknowns of course, but my feelings towards them had shifted into a more accepting place.

The Druids had become amicable towards me, their restricted movements not bothering me as much anymore. The Chimera had returned to the city and resumed their search, but it was business as usual in the Warren. Everyone was doing their part to ensure the safety of every soul who resided in the crystal caves.

Soon, we'd have to go out there and face them, but not until we were ready.

After another particularly unpredictable lesson with Osna—say that ten times fast—I found myself in the kitchens, filling up on every plant-based comfort food I could find.

Arnold's *plat du jour* was some kind of vegetable fritter with a tangy sauce on the side. For sweets was a chocolate pudding, which had the faint tingle of Colour woven into the fluffy bubbles inside the cake— fake Druid chocolate, in other words. It still tasted the same, so it didn't matter either way to me.

I was sitting at a table in the corner when Rory appeared.

"What's that on your hand?" he asked as he sat down. His tray was full as well, since he'd opted for a healthier approach, though he was eying my chocolate pudding.

"Oh." I poked at the rash and grimaced. "Osna is teaching me how certain plants react with skin. She began with nettles and told me that you'd teach me how to use Colour to heal it."

"Oh, did she now?" He poured dressing over his salad. "Made you wait all this time without even giving you ointment, eh?"

"Rory, it stings," I complained.

"Ach, don't be such a baby. Nettles are annoying, not life threatening. Here." He leaned over the table and placed his hand over mine. I felt the warmth of his Colour and the sting immediately went away. "Better?"

"Yes, but how did you do it?"

He wiggled his eyebrows. "*Uruz*, named from the Norse. Mind over matter. Matter over mind."

"There's a lot of Viking in the Druidic runes," I mused, noting he hadn't needed to draw the rune, he'd merely manifested it in his mind. It was a skill I was still working on—sometimes I needed to draw the lines in the air with my finger before more complicated shapes would work, but at least I didn't need to use the stele.

"Or Druid in the Viking," Rory huffed. "Did Osna show you her poison garden?"

I paled. "Poison…garden?"

"Yeah. She's got all kinds of toxic plants hidden down there. If you knew what some of them did, you'd never look at one of Arnold's salads the same way again." He shoved a forkful of said salad into his mouth. "Come to think of it, some you have to handle with gloves."

I scowled at him. "You're being cruel!"

He smirked. "If she teaches you about poisons, that means she likes you."

"I bet she likes you, then."

"Of course, she does!"

A scream sent my heart into overdrive and I shot to my feet, my Colour rising fast. When I saw an oversized lion, with blue streaks through his mane, prowl into the kitchens, I burst into fits of uncontrolled laughter.

Ignis.

Druids scattered in alarm—some fleeing the room entirely—while others stood on chairs, though I wasn't sure what that was supposed to achieve.

Ignis shook out his mane and let out an impressive roar that rattled the dishes stacked on the end of the lunch table. Then he sat in the middle of the room and licked his paws.

"Doesn't that belong to you?" Rory asked, clearly amused. He hadn't moved and was still eating his salad like a lion in the Warren was an everyday occurrence.

"Ignis is his own feline with his own mind," I replied, sitting back down. "There's no owning him."

"He learned a new shape. I wonder how he does it?"

"A warrior's mind is sharp."

"I bet he was vain in his last life," Rory mused. "Just look at the way he's coloured his hair."

"People pay top dollar for that in a salon, I'll have you know."

We laughed as the commotion began to die down.

"You look happy," Rory murmured while everyone was still distracted.

I hesitated. "Do I?"

"For the first time since I met you, you look at ease."

A strange feeling washed over me and I looked at Ignis, who was still preening in the middle of the kitchen, proud of his new shape. Rory was right. I was beginning to feel as if I belonged here. Despite what my father had done, and what future I may bring, I was a Druid. My green hair no longer marked me as an enemy, and my mysterious power was an afterthought to those who'd been teaching me.

I didn't like living in an uncertain world, but for the first time, Rory's words gave me hope that there might be something waiting for me after the prophecy played out.

A home…and a place for me in it.

During that week, I not only realised I had renewed hope for the future, but that I was getting stronger.

Rory began joining Jaimie and I during our evening training sessions. I was glad he was keeping away from that dark portal dungeon and focusing on something else instead. At least for a while.

The two men taught me how to fight, track, conceal, and adapt my abilities to protect. Rory also helped me with my Colour, explaining how the runes Delilah taught me were woven into prisms.

But they were just as clueless as I was when it came to my Fae power. Like me, the Druids only knew of the Chimera and what they'd experienced— their super strength and powers of illusion. Anything else was a bigger mystery than I was.

I'd been thinking about my other half a great deal since my return. The negative energy had come easier than ever the day I used my darker side to save Florence. Phasing was one thing, but drowning Fae in black goop was terrifying. *Where did they go?*

I decided to use it as a last resort, otherwise I wasn't sure what would happen. When I called the darkness, the struggle to contain it was real.

Jaimie's major lesson always stuck with me the most. He said we should use everything we have to our advantage, but not rely heavily on one thing over another. Vanora had the same wisdom and would never allow me to use my Colour whenever she taught me knife skills.

After we'd finished training that evening, Jaimie ditched Rory and I for the kitchens. I swore every time I saw the shapeshifter, he was always complaining he was hungry. His transformations must take a lot out of him, which was something I could understand—I felt much the same way after I used my negative energy, otherwise known as the 'black goop'.

We sat together on the mats as we put our boots back on and my smile faded as I stared at my fingers. They hadn't changed colour, but the memory was still there.

"What?" Rory asked, catching the change in my expression in the mirror.

I almost didn't say anything. "Where do you think they go?"

"Who?"

"When I drown the Chimera in my...*the black goop*...they disappear."

Rory hesitated. "That's a good question. I have no idea."

I snorted. Maybe I sucked them into a hell dimension where they were currently trying to escape so they could exact their terrible revenge on me. Wouldn't that be something?

I picked at my fingernails—a terrible habit—and debated if I should tell Rory about the voices and shadow I'd mistaken for my mother the first time I'd seen it in Calton Cemetery. Normal people would think I was crazy, but I wasn't in the normal world anymore.

I took a deep breath. "When I use my other power, I hear…I hear voices talking to me."

Rory's brow creased. "What do they say?"

I shook my head. "Nothing good."

"And it's only when you use your Fae abilities?"

I nodded. "I feel like I'm talking to myself. Like it's my darker self trying to take control, but then, I'm not sure. Maybe it's someone else hidden within me. Or an elemental entity using my body as a conduit. Sometimes I think it's the prophecy trying to manifest and drag me towards the worst-case scenario."

I thought about the conversation I'd had with it when I was in that field with Florence. *Have you learned nothing from me?*

If the voice was my darker self, then where had my lust for destruction come from? I had plenty of reason to hate the Chimera, after all. They'd hunted my father and me for a quarter of a century, caused no end of pain and suffering to the Druids, and had likely killed my mother because she dared to love my father. If I truly had a darker self, then no wonder I'd drowned so many of the Chimera in my manifestation of negative energy.

But if I could control it and bring it into harmony with my true self, then maybe I could change my destiny and destroy the prophecy once and for all.

"I don't want to accept that this is my only choice," I declared. "That the only way of ending this is to force the black sun to rise on the Druids or the Fae." Delilah said there was good amongst the bad, and if that was true then the only Fae who deserved the black sun were the Chimera. "I want to make my own destiny. I want to do what's right, not what's foretold. If I have to destroy the prophecy, then that's what I'll do."

"I've never heard of a prophecy being destroyed before," Rory said. "They always play out one way or another."

I snorted. "There's a first for everything."

"I don't doubt it."

"What is a prophecy anyway?" I went on. "They only have power if people believe in them."

"Maybe in the human world…"

I rolled my eyes. "It's my prophecy and I refuse it."

"If you say so," Rory said. "It doesn't change the fact that the Chimera are still searching for us. Soon the day will come when we return to the surface."

I didn't need the reminder. "What do you think it is?"

"The voice?"

I nodded.

"It could be as you say, but nothing is certain in this world, Elspeth. Magic can trick you into thinking the complete opposite with little effort. That's why we put so much emphasis on knowing your soul. Your head might trick you, but your soul never will."

His words reminded me of my dream. It could have been the Chimera trying to get to me again, but it could also mean someone was trying to tell me something.

Yenris'del lingers at the World's End. Was it a Fae word? Or had my subconscious muddled a word into an anagram for something else?

"Rory…have you ever heard the world, Yenris'del?"

He screwed up his face. "Yen…ris, what?"

I guessed not. "What about the World's End?"

"The World's End?" He seemed to be confused as to why I was asking but replied, "The World's End was where the original city gate stood. It's about two thirds down the Royal Mile, but no wall stands there now. Pieces of it are about the city, hidden away."

"The Flodden Wall?" I wondered. I remembered seeing pieces of it in Greyfriars.

"Aye. Where the gate used to be is now a pub called *The World's End*. If you look on the road, the humans marked out where it was. It was no wider than a car. Edinburgh was tiny for the amount of people who crammed in here. That's why they built up. The tallest city in the Isles."

"Why did they call it that? The World's End?"

"The city gate was where the world did end for most people," Rory replied. "They never saw outside the walls, and the tall houses and narrow closes were all they ever knew. They couldn't pay the toll to leave, and even if they could, it wasn't a safe time to be wandering Scotland."

"When was this?"

"Ach." He scratched his head. "The sixtieth century? Or there abouts. Why are you asking?"

"I saw it in a dream," I replied absently.

"A dream?"

I told him what I'd seen and how real it felt. I described Greyfriars, the weeping angel and the headstone. Then the Chimera lingering in the shadows who wouldn't answer any of my questions. Finally, I added in the story about Owen attempting to get to me through the same means. I'd told Delilah about it, but I'd ever mentioned it to Rory before.

He looked troubled. "They were in your dreams?"

"Don't worry, I can handle it. Ignis watches over me."

"That's not the point!"

"Do you know anything about keeping Fae out of dreams?" I retorted. "Have you ever had that happen to you?"

He shook his head, his concern not letting up. "Dreams aren't a Druid thing, Elspeth. They've never tried to get to us this way. At least, not that I've heard."

I sighed. "Then it's a Fae thing."

"How many times has this happened?"

"Only twice."

"You don't seem too concerned about it."

"Because I'm not."

Rory sighed and gave me a look that said he thought I was mad. "Elspeth, you're getting stronger, but you're not all-powerful."

"I'm painfully aware of that, thanks," I shot back. "I can't explain it exactly, but I have a *knowing* about things—an intuition—and it hasn't led me astray."

"*Yet.*"

"*Rory*. Seriously!" I threw my hands into the air. "I'm not on your case about your portal research every day, am I?"

He blinked. "Are we having an argument?"

I shook my head and stood. "I hope not, because I'm sorry I brought it up." I was suddenly glad I hadn't mentioned the part where I thought the Chimera wanted to possess my subconscious. Not that I knew he could for sure—he could've been trying to scare me.

"All right." Rory shrugged and looked up at me. "See you tomorrow, then."

As I walked through the Warren, my mind lingered on the dream once more…and the random observation that I'd never seen a female Chimera.

I was getting the feeling I was being invited—or lured—to the World's End.

The Chimera had gotten into my dreams before and it had certainly crossed my mind that this might all be an elaborate trap. I didn't know anyone else who might want to send me a message. Before the Druids, I was alone in the world. There was no one out there for me…or was there? My mother might still be alive, right? I didn't dare to hope.

Sighing, I put it out of my mind. After another busy day, I was exhausted and if I kept puzzling over it, I'd never get to sleep.

When I opened the door to my room, I found Ignis stretched out on the bed like a banana. He'd returned to his house cat shape, though he'd decided to keep his glorious lion's mane.

It was such a hilarious sight, I forgot all about the World's End, dreams, and the unknown Yenris'del, and collapsed onto my bed in fits of laughter.

I was safe in the Warren, especially when I was asleep. I had a magical cat as my guardian, after all.

12

Both Rory and I had cooled down by the next morning.

I waited for the Druid in the library, gazing at the crystal ceiling. Ignis had wandered off an hour ago, content to entertain himself for the day, so I was alone with my thoughts until the door banged open.

My heart skipped several beats and I turned to see Rory sauntering into the room.

He'd ditched his usual battered jeans and T-shirt in favour of a slouchy V-neck T-shirt—that showed his manly cleavage—black trousers, and combat boots. Had he dressed up? Well, that was a bit of an overstatement, but he had made *some* improvement.

I noticed he wore his knife at his left hip, something he hadn't been doing since he was ordered to stay in the Warren and teach me the mysterious ways of Druidic Colour. Something was up, and it didn't have anything to do with his hipster fashion sense.

I raised my eyebrows, noticing the faint outline of a rune tattooed over his heart.

"How do I look?" Rory asked, fishing for a compliment.

"Like you're a hipster who stepped out of the early noughties and forgot to complete your look with a man bun."

His cheeks flushed and he threw his arms into the air. "Try to impress a bonnie lass and what do I get? The cheek of you!"

"What's that?" I asked, forgetting myself and pulling at the neck of his T-shirt. Realising what I'd done, I jerked my hand away.

"Aye," Rory murmured, his tone turning serious, though the colour in his cheeks didn't go away. He pressed his palm over the rune. "*Mo chridhe trom s'dulaich.*" My heart is heavy.

"Oh… I-I didn't know you had any."

"It's a protection rune, no more," he added. "I've had it for years."

What did he want to protect his heart from? My gaze flickered back to the edge of the rune unbidden. Perhaps it was the pain of losing his parents, or a lost love. *Or Vanora*, a small voice taunted.

Awkward silence opened between us and I looked at his knife. Desperate to change the subject, I asked, "What are we doing today?"

"We're going up to the city on patrol," he told me.

My heart skipped a beat. I'd become used to the closed safety of the Warren and the thought of the outside world had me on edge. The Elders had spoken about the return of the Chimera, and it seemed risky to go up there knowing the Fae were waiting for an opportunity to grab me…and anyone else who might stand by my side.

"Are you sure?" I asked. "If I phase into the city, the Chimera will know we're lurking."

"I'm sure and the Chimera always lurk. We're all creepy lurkers," Rory replied breezily. "Are *you* sure?"

My palm settled on the hilt of the knife at my waist. I'd began wearing it every day, from the time I got up until I went to bed, so I'd become used to feeling its weight. It was another of Vanora's barked commands. If I wanted to be a warrior, I had to act like one.

"Don't be tricked by the safety of the Warren, Elspeth," Rory added. "You can't get too comfortable down here, otherwise you might lose your bite."

"My bite?"

"Aye. You've faced the Chimera several times and won. That takes bite, lass. If it's courage you're looking for, you've got plenty."

I drew in a deep breath, allowing my thoughts to settle as my lungs filled to the brim. If we are going to defeat the Chimera, then I'd have to go out there and face them sooner or later. The past few weeks were all about preparing me for this moment…leaving the

Warren and becoming a warrior—a *curaidh*—for the Druids.

Besides, it wasn't like a swarm of Fae had taken over humanity and were waiting in the city. I hadn't been underground *that* long.

"Okay," I said. "Where do you want me to take us?"

Rory gave me a look.

"What? You thought we were going the long way?"

"A portal isn't the long way," he complained.

"It is when I can teleport."

He scratched his head. "Aye, you can teleport. How far can you go?"

I shrugged. "If you want to go somewhere in the city, that's no problem. The farthest I've gone a few hundred miles."

His eyes widened. "A few hundred miles?"

I laughed and knocked my shoulder against his. "Imagine the money I'll save on airfare. No more lining up at airport security for me!"

"You're environmentally friendly, that's for sure. Can you take two at once?"

I nodded. "So where to, *neach-gleidhidh*?"

"Holyrood," he replied. "At the bottom of Arthur's Seat, if you please."

I grinned and grabbed his hand. "You've got it."

"Should I hold your other hand?" he asked, suddenly looking pale. "For insurance purposes."

"Raurich Maerinn-Mackenzie, are you afraid of phasing?"

"Ach, no I'm not, Elspeth Odhweine-Quarrie," he said with a pout. "Let's go."

I stifled a smile and took his other hand. Before he could stop me again, I pictured Arthur's Seat and the outer fence of the Holyrood Palace gardens. Then I phased.

It only took the blink of an eye to leave the Warren and appear on the surface.

We landed, our boots touching the ground with a gentle tap. I puffed out my chest, pleased that I was getting better at the landing part. Seeing Rory fall on his arse would be funny, but I doubted he'd see it the same way. The Druid's pride was bigger than his head sometimes.

"*Ach.*" Rory shivered and shook out his arms. "I felt like my insides were turning inside out. How can you stand it?"

"It doesn't feel like anything to me." I offered him a reassuring smile and looked around, but I couldn't sense any Fae.

I looked up at the sky, blinking in the sunlight. Unbroken blue stretched from horizon to horizon and my breath caught. The colours slicing through the ancient volcanic cliffs of Arthur's Seat were spectacular, though tourists were climbing the winding paths in a thick stream, desperate to get their selfies at the top.

"Where did the rain go?" I wondered out loud.

"Summer came while you were underground," Rory said, chuckling at my reaction. It was if I'd never experienced summer before, but everyone knew the same season in Australia could be brutally hot. This was nothing I couldn't handle.

I felt the sun attempt to burn my pale nose and I lifted a hand to shield my eyes. "I always imagined Scotland to be forever overcast with a ninety-five percent chance of rain."

"Aye, Summer doesn't last long," he told me. "At the first sign of blue skies, everyone's in shorts and T-shirts, and having picnics in the Princes Street Gardens. You can't see the grass for all the blankets."

I imagined a sea of tartan, wicker baskets, and sandwiches. "It actually sounds nice."

"Aye, it is. Sunglasses are a must. The glare reflecting off every Scot's pasty white skin is blinding."

I snorted. "Just be grateful you're not in Australia. Your hipster man chest would burn to a crisp ten times faster."

He ignored my cheap insult. "Maybe one day we can go together."

I looked up at him. "To Australia?"

He shrugged. "Aye, why not?"

It was the first time he'd talked about what came after the Chimera, and not in terms of the Darklands. To be honest, I was surprised he thought about anything else.

"Home always seems so boring compared to

other places," I mused. "It's not until you visit it with someone else that you realise how special it can be."

"I feel that way about Edinburgh sometimes," Rory admitted. "Though now that I'm here with you…" His demeanour turned a little melancholy around the edges.

I wondered if he was having second-thoughts about his portal research. If he was successful, the Druids would have to decide if they wanted to brave the Darklands in order to reach the homeland. Not even my father had found the way back, but if Rory did…

"Do you want to leave Scotland?" I asked.

The Druid snorted but didn't reply.

I wanted to ask him if he would stay if the Chimera were gone, but I knew better than to push. I kept quiet, watching his changing expression as a light breeze buffeted my green hair.

"Let's walk up the Mile," he said after a moment. "I can show you the World's End."

As we walked, he explained how the Druids moved through the city. I already knew how to use the slightest of illusions to mask our presence but looking for the signs the Fae had passed, or were lurking, were new to me.

When I was out on my own, I could sense them when they were approaching. Their nearness was like a chill trembling across my skin, but I hadn't figured out a way to tell where they'd been or how they got there. That's where Rory stepped in and filled in some of the blanks.

He showed me strange curved symbols hidden along the Mile—calling cards left by the Chimera. What they meant was a mystery, but their existence was clear enough.

The faintest touch of Colour showed us old paths well-travelled by the enemy, footprints and traces of a sickly-sweet scent that reminded me of rot. Scanning the people on the streets revealed nothing but humans enjoying the warm summer day, though peeling away the layers of complex illusions was something I'd come to understand and see in person more times than I cared for.

Edinburgh was peeling back and showing me a whole new layer I hadn't imagined existed. The world of the Fae, no matter how small their presence was here, was interwoven so densely with humanity I could be forgiven for not noticing until now.

"Ever since the Witches opened their portals, the Fae have spread across the Irish Sea," Rory explained. "Some of these traces aren't just Chimera."

"I know, you've told me this."

"Most were happy to go back to their own world, but others weren't," he went on, ignoring me. "Earth is the only home they knew, and their homeland is as alien to them as it is to us."

"Then why haven't we seen any?"

"The Chimera drive many into hiding. Whatever their politics are, it's clear they aren't the good guys in their world, either. What I've taught you is the sum of everything we know, and it is next to nothing. Whatever your father learned from his time in their world passed with him."

He was right. Not even his journal had shed much light on the ways of the Fae, and neither had the vision his tears conjured—except for the golden-haired, feline Fae who'd helped him escape with me. She was just as much of a mystery as my mother was.

I grimaced and looked sideways at *Campbell's Serviced Apartments*. Rory had sliced the original Mrs. Campbell open from neck to navel, spilling her Chimera guts all over the foyer. Now a new Mrs. Campbell ran the apartments, which were a front for a shady operation of lure and capture. I'd almost been the biggest prize of all.

"They're still in there," Rory said, following my gaze.

"Can they see us?" I asked.

"Not unless they make direct eye contact."

I shivered and blew through my lips. "She was replaced so easily…like nothing ever happened."

"Life has a different meaning to them." Rory threaded his arm through mine and steered me away from the apartments. "Ethics need not apply."

I didn't like the sound of that. It meant nothing was off limits in the fight to come.

The World's End pub sat on the corner of the Royal Mile and St. Mary's Street. Four dreary grey floors sat above it, though the pub itself was painted a deep cobalt blue and had bright gold signage. Cheery flowers grew in pots that hung between each window, and the historic story of the area's origins had been painstakingly painted on the wall near the street corner.

We stood on the opposite footpath, outside of another pub—this one was painted maroon—and the Celtic jewellery store that sat beside it.

Studying the World's End, I came to the conclusion that there wasn't anything special about it. I sensed nothing magical in the air, saw no runes, or felt a single chill. I did smell the faint tang of barely and hops as the pub door opened and closed, but all pubs smelled like that—beer, cooking food, and earthy woodsmoke.

If the World's End was so important, why was it in my dream?

A close ran behind the pub, stretching through the tall shadows between buildings. I stared past the arched opening and into the depths, blinking as the alley seemed to grow and stretch into forever like a vortex to another world.

I shook my head, my equilibrium knocked a little sideways, and Rory glanced back at me.

"What is it?" he asked.

"That close."

He followed my pointing finger and frowned. "What about it?"

"It was like it grew…" I paled as I realised he couldn't see or sense everything I did. "Do you think there are only things I can see because I'm half-Fae?"

"Probably," he replied. "Have you seen anything else like that?"

I shook my head, then gasped. "Greyfriars," I told him. "The day I first got here. The same thing happened right before the Chimera appeared."

"Interesting."

"Is that why you brought me up here?"

"Your powers are growing every day, Elspeth. It stands to reason that you'd see things that weren't meant for Druid eyes."

"You didn't answer my question."

"A little of column A, a little of column B."

I slapped him on the back of the head.

"Ow!" he cried. "What was that for?"

"Could've told me."

Looking at the close again, I couldn't get past the feeling that something was drawing me to this place. There was nothing here, which made it all the stranger. But I did know that whatever was lingering at the World's End, the Chimera were watching it.

"What could it be?" I asked Rory. "The thing in the close?"

"Could be nothing," he replied. "Or it could be something. Whatever you saw, *if it was something*, it wasn't meant for me." He pulled me out of the way of a rowdy group of tourists and we stood at the edge of the road, staring at the pub. "Is this about those dreams you had?"

"Yeah. I thought if I saw it, it might make sense. But," I frowned, "there's nothing here."

"Be careful," he warned. "The Chimera a cunning. They could be using our lack of knowledge about your Fae heritage to their advantage."

"That's what I thought."

I pushed it to the back of my mind and looked down at the bricks marking the original city gate. Rory was right. It was a tiny opening at best.

If the Chimera were calling out to me, they'd try again. If it was someone else—another Fae—then they'd try again. Both of them would, and I'd figure out if friend or foe waited at the World's End.

"C'mon," Rory said. "We've got a lot of ground to cover."

"How long does patrol last for?"

"As long as it takes to check in to all our markers."

"And how many of them are there?"

"Fifteen."

"*Fifteen?*" I sighed dramatically.

"What do you think we'd be doing? Drinking pints at the pub?" Rory chuckled. "That's why Darby has been pushing you so hard. Endurance matters."

"You do realise I was always picked last in PhysEd at school, right? I couldn't catch a ball for the life of me."

He leaned close and winked. "And now you'll always be picked first."

Flushing, I swatted him away. "Let's keep going then. I don't like lingering out in the open."

The Druid's way of patrolling seemed rather loose, but the more I thought about our trip through the city, the more I realised it was *his* style. If I were here with Jaimie or Vanora, we wouldn't be talking openly about Fae on the street corner. Rory had a happy-go-lucky way about him that unsettled me at times, considering what we were up against.

"Aye," he said. "This way. Keep your eyes peeled."

13

———

Vanora was waiting for me when I turned up to our practice session the next morning.

The blisters on my toes had blisters and I winced as my boots rubbed against them. I could use a little Colour to get rid of them, but I wanted to adhere to the teachings of the Druids and not use magic to fix all my problems…no matter how minor.

The Druidess glared at me, but that wasn't anything new. Our relationship hadn't progressed past the point of frosty tolerance, though me being half-Fae no longer had anything to do with it.

"What did you say to Rory?" she demanded, crossing her arms over her chest.

I screwed up my face. "Excuse me?"

"You heard me."

I bristled. She must still be on Rory's case about his portal research, because I couldn't think of anything else I'd done. I thought he'd stopped while we'd been training, but from the look of rage on Vanora's face, apparently not.

"I didn't say anything he didn't need to hear about his stupid portals, if that's what you're referring to," I told her. There was only so much I *could* say to him—after all, he was a grown adult who could make his own choices.

"When you came back from patrol yesterday, he was different," she snapped. "What did you say to him?"

"Nothing, I—" We'd been talking about Edinburgh and how it looked different through new eyes. *I feel that way about Edinburgh sometimes. Though now that I'm here with you...* One thing I'd learned about Rory was that he was a master at concealing his true feelings.

Vanora sighed and rolled her eyes at me. "You did say something. *I knew it.*"

"I don't know," I admitted. "He seemed sad."

"Sad?" Her feline eyes studied me with a coolness that cut into my soul.

"I don't know," I said again. "You know him better than I do. He hides things with humour and muddles my head with his Druidic witticisms."

"Well, the moment he got back yesterday, he went into that hole of his and hasn't come out since. I went in there, but he threw me out!" She swept her hand through the air. "Swore like a *muc salach.*"

"That doesn't sound like Rory."

"He's been different ever since you came here."

I opened my mouth to retort, but a loud crash boomed through the Warren. We both turned towards the door, our argument forgotten.

"What was that?" I asked.

Vanora unsheathed her knife. "Nothing good."

A ripple fluttered through the air and I glanced at the Druidess. "It's not Fae."

"Aye. It's not Druid, either."

She opened the door and stepped out into the hall, but the moment she turned, a black shadow rushed past and knocked her flying. I gasped as the sound of thumping footsteps faded and rushed to the Druidess.

Vanora was on the floor, out cold. Her knife had skidded across the turquoise and obsidian tunnel, and her immaculate braid had come loose. I fell to my knees beside her and pressed my palm to her forehead. My Colour bloomed and pulsed through her body.

Her heart was beating and her lungs filled with air. She was unconscious, but okay.

I glanced up and down the tunnel, the sounds of screaming Druids echoed through the Warren. Whatever that thing was, it wasn't friendly.

I glanced down at Vanora. I couldn't leave her here—no matter how frosty we were to one another.

Sighing, I grabbed her knife and thrust it back into the scabbard at her hip, then scrambled to my feet. Hooking my hands underneath her shoulders, I dragged her back into the training room, my muscles straining with the effort. *Damn, she was heavier than she looked.*

I closed her inside the room and took off down the hall, drawing my knife. Passing a few startled and slightly injured Druids, they all pointed me in the same direction—the main cavern.

I hurtled through the winding tunnel and shot out into the open space.

Salle shuddered as something large rammed into the trunk. Leaves shook free, fluttering wildly through the air. I skidded to a halt as the shadow leapt out from behind the tree and I almost peed myself at the sight of it.

It was an enormous, black wolf.

My hands shook as I stared up at the creature while it prowled towards me. It had to be twice my height and then some. I'd never seen anything like it. Was this another attack by the Chimera?

The wolf aimed its glowing red eyes at me as more Druids ran into the cavern. The rotting stench radiating from its jaws had a pile of vomit quickly rise to my throat. Rows upon rows of sharp teeth connected to an elongated snout, which joined with an impossibly large head with pointed ears. Then there was the black fur and claws—each one was as long as my fingers.

Swallowing hard, I tightened my grip on my knife. *I was going to need a bigger weapon.*

"Elspeth," Darby murmured from somewhere

behind me, *"don't move."* She didn't have to tell me twice.

The wolf lowered its head and growled, the sound dragging against my mind. Wherever it had come from, the creature held some kind of power and was attempting to use it.

Something told me we were in a battle of animalistic dominance and I didn't dare break eye contact with it in case it meant something I couldn't take back.

Druids lined up behind me, their Colour reverberating through the cavern.

"Don't break eye contact," Rowen told me. "It's the only thing stopping it from attacking."

"Why does it want me?" I murmured. "Maybe I look like a tasty sausage with a bit of lettuce on top."

"It sees you as the alpha," Shor said in a clipped tone. His pride was hurt, but I got that vibe from the Elder all the time.

"Are we really going to have an argument about gender equality right now?" I hissed. "It wants to rip my head off."

"Stay cool, lass." Jaimie was right behind me. I doubted his German Shepard form could stand against a giant wolf, but his strength was sorely needed.

Everyone was here except for Vanora and Rory. *Rory.*

"It came from below," Delilah said.

I cursed in Gaelic, finding an unknown

understanding of the most foul swear words to grace the language.

"Ach, *lass*," Jaimie muttered.

"We have to lure it to the workshop," I told the others. "Then, force it back through the portal."

"Portal?" Darby asked.

The wolf bared its teeth and snapped, its rancid jaws coming within an inch of my face. I shuddered but held my ground. *I think I just shat myself.*

I sifted through my rambling throughs, trying to make sense through the fear that threatened to overwhelm me.

The tunnels down there weren't large enough for it to fit, which meant the wolf had more magic at its disposal. It was a primal predator…a hunter.

My darkness stirred and I held up my hand, the other returning my knife to its scabbard. "It will chase me. I'll lead it back to the portal, but I'll need help keeping it on course."

"We're with you," Rowen said. "We'll guard the path. Delilah?"

"Leave the portal to me," my grandmother murmured.

The wolf lowered its head and its ears flattened. There was no more time.

"Now!" I shouted.

The Druids scattered and I took off, sprinting across the cavern, around *Salle*, and into a tunnel. The wolf followed, howling as if it called for its pack, and thank goodness, it was the only one here.

I skidded around the corner, my boots almost losing their grip on the glossy crystal floor. I glanced over my shoulder, and as I had hoped, the wolf changed its shape to fit inside the tunnel behind me.

Cursing, I lengthened my stride, silently thanking Darby—something I never thought would happen in a million years—for pushing me so hard.

I turned down another tunnel and the wolf broke away, but a Druid was there to buffet it back on course. It crashed into a prismatic web of thick Colour, howled, and resumed its chase.

If someone had asked me where I saw myself after I'd graduated university, this was the last place I would've imaged. Running through a crystal cave, being chased by what could only be described as a hellhound, sounded more like the opening of a fantasy novel than actual reality.

Colour flared behind me, but I didn't dare look back. A few more turns and I would be there.

I swallowed hard. *What if Rory was dead?* What would I do if I ran in there and saw him torn apart on the floor?

My heart was beating so fast, I thought it was going to burst from my chest. The wolf's thundering gait crashed behind me, incredibly loud and impossibly close.

Run, Elspeth. Don't lose your nerve now.

I sailed around the final corner and crashed into the workshop, leaping over the splintered door, my lungs almost at critical mass.

Rory's portal flickered in the centre of the room, only barely holding its form. I spotted the Druid lying in the corner, groaning and clutching his head, but there was no time to be thankful...*or mad.*

I darted around the portal, but the wolf skidded to a stop and snapped at the air. It was intelligent enough to know this world was better than the one it came from.

Rory moaned and the creature's eyes fixed on him.

"*Hey,*" I shouted, unsheathing my knife. "*Over here.*" The wolf turned its head and its red eyes found mine. "That's it." I began to edge around the room, attempting to get its back facing the portal. My breath burned as I heaved in gulps of oxygen between clipped sentences. "Focus on me. The alpha. Kill me and you'll have power over the pack. That's how it works, right?"

The wolf bared its teeth and I wondered if it understood what I said. The glint in its red eyes told me it just might.

My darkness fought against my Colour, desperate to take control. I felt my fingers tighten as my power rose and the wolf's growl deepened. I knew black goop had coated my knife and dripped to the floor—a warning the beast took loud and clear.

I raised my arms as my skin lost its warmth, standing on the precipice of letting go. All I had to do was relax and my evil self would take over and fix everything. *The black sun would send this beast back to the Hell in which it came from…*

"Easy, granddaughter." Delilah's presence brightened the shadows as she entered the workshop behind me. "We must send it back to the world it came from."

The portal stabilised and opened with a whoosh, the blast of energy threw papers around the room.

Beyond the ripping surface, I could see a world of fire and ash that looked a lot like Hell. A red sky burned over a blackened forest and a river of molten rock flowed into a valley beyond.

Heat blasted my face and I pushed the wolf toward the portal with everything I had as Delilah held the way open. Colour, negative energy, physical strength— it all piled against the beast as it began to grow again.

I wasn't strong enough…not without letting my Fae blood loose.

I dropped my knife and a rasped cry tore from my lips. I lunged and collided with the enormous wolf. Prisms splintered from my skin, crystallising as I wrapped my arms around its neck.

We tumbled through the portal and the creature howled with rage. Searing heat encased me like I'd fallen into the heart of a furnace and my skin began to blister. We tore apart and I rolled once before I settled on my feet.

I gasped for air, the Sulphur-rich atmosphere sucking the oxygen out of my lungs.

The wolf howled and righted itself, then sprinted back towards me and the portal.

"*Elspeth!*"

I turned blindly and grasped the hand that stretched towards me. A powerful tug propelled my body through the portal and back into the Warren. I fell to the floor, gasping for breath as a snap shut the way closed.

"Are you all right?" Delilah kneeled beside me, her hands working prisms across my blistered skin.

Two seconds in an inhospitable world had almost killed me. Now I understood the real danger of what my father, and now Rory, were facing in their search for the Darklands.

I glanced down at my hands; they were back to normal—the back goop was gone, as was the blue sheen. The blisters the harsh atmosphere burned on my exposed flesh absorbed back into my body thanks to Delilah's Colours.

"Yeah." My gaze fixed on Rory, who was staring at us in shock. "I'm okay."

The Druid coughed and wiped at his eyes, clearly distressed and ashamed.

Delilah looked at Rory, then to me.

"I need to tend to the injured," she said, narrowing her eyes at him. "The Elders will speak with you in due course, Raurich. This reckless endangerment and unauthorised use of Colour cannot go unpunished."

"Unauthorised?" I exclaimed. "You mean, all this time—"

Delilah held up a hand to quiet my protest. She said nothing before leaving, but her silence was worse than saying anything and everything. Even I felt sick and hoped I never got on her bad side.

I glared at Rory, who was rubbing his sleeve over a bleeding cut on his head, and I picked up my knife. I made a show of sliding it back into my scabbard while my anger simmered.

Then I unleashed.

"Why would you be so reckless?" I raged. "You let a monster from a hell dimension into the Warren!"

"I know."

"It almost killed me!"

"*I'm sorry.*"

"You're supposed to be a guardian, Rory. Why—"

"I said, I know," he hissed.

"Why can't you see that this is dangerous? Did anything I say to you sink in?"

"Fighting the Chimera is dangerous," he argued.

"Fighting the Chimera is *necessary.*" I jabbed a finger to where the portal had opened. "That isn't. It isn't even *authorised!*"

Rory fisted his hands into his hair and let out a strangled cry. "I want to go home!" he shouted. "There has to be more to life than this!"

"Than what?" I demanded. "The Warren? From where I'm standing, it's a pretty great home, Rory."

"We hide who we are, Elspeth. We can't live

openly. What do you think will happen the moment we go outside and reveal ourselves to humanity?"

"Oh, I have a pretty good idea," I scoffed.

"*We don't belong in this world*. Why should we protect it?"

I shook my head. "Because, for better or worse, it's our home. It's the only one you've ever known, and the only one I have now that my father is dead. *Have a little respect*."

"Elspeth—"

"Your obsession is going to get us killed and the Chimera will thank you for it."

He closed his mouth with a snap and leaned against the table.

"With power comes responsibility," I told him. "Protecting the Warren and the Druids who live in it is that responsibility, Rory. Life will never be easy for people like us. This may not be *Thríbhís Mhór*, but it's the next best thing."

He laughed and pressed his bloodied sleeve against his head.

"What?" I demanded.

"Isn't it ironic that you finally get what I've been trying to drill into your head since the day we met, and now I'm the one who's refusing to believe it?"

He pushed off the table and stood in front of me.

"You can't open another portal," I said. "I know you want to find the homeland, but it can't be like this. Not now."

In true Rory fashion, he wasn't listening.

"You were…" He drew in a shaking breath. "You fought that beast like…*a sheòid.*"

Before I realised what was happening, his lips met mine in a hard, passionate kiss.

I jerked back like I'd been shocked and slapped him. My palm cracked against his face, the blow stinging my skin. Rory blinked and pressed his hand over the reddening mark, his eyes hazy with bewilderment.

"*You pig!*" We turned to see Vanora stand just inside the door with an expression of pure rage. She shrieked at him again—this time in Gaelic, which was too foul to repeat—and picked up shards of quartz before she hurled them at the Druid.

I darted out of the way as he shielded himself from her onslaught. Crystal collided with the wall, shattering into sharp splinters.

"Ach, Vanora!" he cried. "*Air do shocair! Stad!*"

"*Pig!*" She hurled some more quartz clusters with alarming force.

Sighing, I decided it was best to leave them alone and go help Delilah. Rory had earned his punishment, and then some. A few crystal splinters were a small price to pay for the mayhem he'd caused today.

Out in the hall, I pressed my fingers to my lips.

14

I barely slept that night.

Ignis had been absent during the chaos with the wolf, but he made up for it by trying to sit as close to me as he could possibly get. If it meant sitting on my stomach and staring at me while I tried to sleep, then that's what he did.

"*Ignis*," I complained, shoving him off.

He let out a meow of protest and sat beside me, his tail flicking back and forth.

A sheòid… A warrior.

I didn't know what to think about the wolf marking me as the alpha. I certainly didn't feel like I had that kind of power amongst the Druids, especially standing beside the Elders.

Finally, I sat up with a grunt of frustration and rubbed my tired eyes. I was getting nowhere trying to fall asleep—there was too much on my mind for any sort of calm.

Yenris'del lingers at the World's End. Maybe it wasn't as literal as it sounded. The World's End could also mean the place where life ended.

Maybe I'd find some answers in death. If I went to the same place, but in the spirit world, there could be a chance I'd see the part of the puzzle I was missing. I didn't have anything else to go on.

"You wanna go for a walk?" I asked Ignis. "I think it's time to push a little harder for some information, don't you think?"

He blinked slowly in an attempt to hypnotise me and I laughed. He disapproved but would come anyway.

Sliding out of bed, I pulled on a jumper and my boots, even though it didn't matter what I wore. There was no feeling on the other side, at least none that I'd ever felt before.

Grasping my stele, I etched some runes of protection in a circle on the floor. Colour flared as each symbol completed, settling onto the turquoise and obsidian stone like a delicate strand of glittering spiderweb. *I'd never get tired of seeing runes form.*

I stood in the middle of the circle, took a deep breath, and summoned the veil. Then, I stepped forwards.

Opening my eyes, the mists of death curled around my ankles. My room had dissolved, leaving me floating in an endless void of grey.

The tiger Ignis sat beside me, watching the mist with sharp eyes.

I'd only come here twice before—once to see my father, and the second, when I learned more about Ignis's past—so I wasn't quite sure what I was looking for.

Answers were waiting here, more than the ones I sought, and I sharpened my mind in an attempt to hear some of them.

Whispers tickled my ears and I turned, searching for the source, but no one was there. Their words were too faint to make out. Ignis looked up at me, his tiger eyes glinting in monochrome. He heard them, too.

Interesting. Spirits seemed to linger here on their way to other places. The afterlife perhaps? Thoughts of everything from reincarnation and hauntings came to mind and I wondered if death was meant to be that layered. Life was complicated enough without the option to remain or become trapped in a place as featureless as this.

I could feel them now. The currents that bound our passage to the next life.

"Death is so like a train station," I murmured. "The currents are the tracks and the souls are the trains." I snorted at the analogy and shook my head.

Awareness was a strange thing in a place with no colour or feeling. The sharper my senses became, the more I saw.

The air rippled and shapes formed through the haze. At first, they were indistinguishable from ripples on the surface of a lake—soft waves that ebbed and flowed with absent wind currents—but the closer I ventured, the clearer they became.

Featureless faces pushed against an unseen barrier, screaming and clawing in a desperate attempt to get out of wherever death had stowed them away. There were three, then four, then six...and I recognised them all.

Ignis growled in warning, but I wasn't afraid.

They were echoes of the Chimera I'd fought and killed in life, but were they of my making or a natural phenomena of the limbo in which we now stood?

I stepped closer and the voices rose; hands and faces pushed against the barrier with more force. Shivering, I moved back.

I couldn't sense Owen at all. Maybe he'd already passed on, but... But what if he hadn't come here at all? What if what I'd done to him was the same thing that had almost happened to Ignis? *Erasure.*

I threaded my fingers through the tufts of hair around the tiger's ears, taking comfort in his presence. This place was cold and unfeeling—death didn't discriminate. All were equal in the icy reaches of the void in-between.

"The World's End," I whispered, turning away from the Fae. Maybe if I said it, it would help us find it.

As we walked, the mist parted and allowed us through. More shapes began to emerge from the grey —sharp lines and angles, the dip of a gutter, the depression of a window or two, a street sign, a set of traffic lights, and the darkened opening of a narrow close.

I stood before the arch with Ignis at my side and we stared down the small lane, but even in death, the path was closed. It stretched and shimmered, disappearing into forever.

It was the same phenomena I'd seen in life. I knew, with it present here, it was a sign that I'd been on the right track...but I was missing something. A key, or a magic word... No matter how silly it sounded, perhaps the Fae had their own arcane tricks.

Delilah had told me in one of her lessons that there were tricksters amongst their kind. Creatures who thrived on illusion and subterfuge to get what they wanted...or for the sheer pleasure of causing mayhem.

Rory had warned me about the Chimera laying traps for me, but what if someone was laying a trap for the Chimera over a path that was meant only for me? What if the answers I was looking for lay beneath the illusion?

I had to go to the World's End and see for myself. It was the only way forwards I could see, and it had to be as soon as possible.

"No risk, no reward," I whispered as Ignis and I turned back towards life.

The next morning, I gathered my courage and went to see Rory. After looking everywhere, I found him in his workshop, licking his wounds—and cleaning up the mess with a rather bedraggled straw broom.

My stomach churned as I lingered in the doorway, completely unnoticed. *Man, I hated confrontation.*

Broken quartz tinkled as he swept it into little piles, his movements slow and unenthusiastic. He sighed at intervals, leaning on the broom for a moment before he resumed his work.

Finally, I couldn't handle it anymore and stepped into the room. "So, what punishment did they give you?"

Rory looked up from his broom, startled. When he saw me, his spirits seemed to brighten and my lips tingled with the memory of the day before. Strange that was the thing that stuck in my mind the most, rather than the giant wolf and the near-death experience in an oxygen-deprived alternate reality.

"Hey," he murmured. "Are you okay?"

I raised my eyebrows and glanced at the piles of shattered quartz. "Are you?"

"Ach, a few scratches and a bump on the head." His gaze turned towards where the portal had opened.

"I'm fine," I said a little too bluntly. I was the eye of the storm wherever I went. "What did the Elders say?"

His cheeks reddened, melting a little of my anger

towards him. It wasn't like him to be ashamed or embarrassed.

"I'm not allowed to leave the Warren or continue my research," he told me. "If there was a prison, I'd be in it. I'm surprised they didn't build one especially for me."

I grunted. The Druids were a peaceful people, so this seemed unprecedented. How did they punish when they hadn't had to punish before? Apart from me punching on with Darby, this seemed to be a first —though I didn't know what happened after the incident with the mob and my attempted murder. Honestly, I didn't want to go there.

"Have you seen Vanora?" he asked. "She won't speak to me."

I snorted. "No."

Rory sighed. "Elspeth—"

I held up my hand. *"Don't."*

"But—"

"You do understand that we can't be together, right?"

Narrowing his eyes, he replied, "No. I don't see why."

"I'm half-Fae and wrapped up in a prophecy of death. There's every likelihood that I'll die trying to stop it, and if I don't, I will never risk bringing a child into this world who is even remotely like me. Besides, I will never be welcome in the homeland, Rory. I'm not a pure-blooded Druid. I could never go with you. Is your birthright something you're willing to give up?" I shook my head. "I couldn't live with myself if I took that choice from you."

"Well, you went from zero to ten thousand in less than a second," he drawled. "You won't even give it any thought?"

I scowled. "I have given it a lot of thought."

"A single night isn't any time at all."

"Vanora loves you," I blurted, my heart twisting. "It's more than a genetic match to her. I'm shiny and new, but it won't be long before I dull. You should give her a chance."

He stared at me like I'd slapped him for a second time. He hadn't bothered to ask how I felt about him, while pressing me to accept his advances, so I didn't feel bad. 'Giving it thought' wasn't exactly the same thing.

"I tried to love her," he murmured, "before you came. But I couldn't force what wasn't there." He closed his eyes for a moment. "This isn't a choice between you or her, Elspeth. She knows how I feel. Should I stop living my life because she can't let go?"

I narrowed my eyes. How would I know? I'd never had a boyfriend stick around for more than a couple of weeks, let alone know what real love felt like. Of course, I wanted it, but only if it was returned.

I thought about Rory and Vanora's genetic partnership and knew it would cause more pain in the long run. How could the Elders decree such a thing? Was the survival of the Darkland Druids that important?

"And what about the child you are duty bound to bring into the world?" I asked, not able to keep my mouth shut. *Good work, Elspeth. Especially since you need to ask him for a favour.*

Rory's expression twisted in pain. "I don't want to do it," he admitted. "I never wanted to for so many reasons…" The workshop fell silent.

I regretted asking and wished I had the power to turn back time for thirty seconds. We needed a change of subject, and stat.

"About the portal," I began, but Rory groaned and shook his head.

"I'm so sorry," he blurted. "I knew it was dangerous, but nothing was meant to come through, I—"

"You owe me one," I interrupted before he decided to get onto his knees and beg. "Now it's time to pay up."

He blinked. "Already?"

"Times are tough. I need answers and I know where to find them. You're going to help me get to them."

"Answers? Where?"

"The Elders will never sanction me going out into the city to look for Fae," I said. "So, I have to take matters into my own hands."

"Hold on. You want to look for Fae? In Edinburgh? Right now? Without permission?"

I nodded. "And you're coming with me."

"You're kidding, right?" He shook his head. "The

Elders will roast me alive if I leave. I'm lucky they didn't already exile me."

"I don't intend to get caught. If we do, then they'll understand."

He sighed and began to pace, weaving a trail around the piles of quartz. "But how do you know where to go? Who are you looking for? If you want me to hunt Chimera, then it's a flat-out no." He swept his hand through the air, making a cutting motion. "I know you want answers—*we all do*—but that's a hard limit, Elspeth."

"As hard a limit as opening portals to hell dimensions?"

He stopped his pacing and glared at me. "Ach, too soon."

"Remember when I told you about those dreams?" I asked, ignoring him. "Well, someone was trying to leave me a message."

"What message?"

"Yenris'del lingers at the World's End."

Rory sighed again. "I didn't know it was that important; otherwise, we could have looked a little harder the other day…even though I couldn't see anything."

"I didn't know for sure," I retorted. "A lot of this stuff still goes over my head, you know. Anyway, Ignis and I went into death last night and confirmed it. Someone's looking for me and they're not Chimera. They're just trying to hijack the connection to stop whoever it is who wants to talk to me. That means it's important, right?"

Rory slashed his hand through the air again. "It doesn't matter. It could be a trap."

"The thought crossed my mind, but what if it isn't? We're short on answers, Rory. I can't keep pushing my abilities and not understand what I'm unleashing, not when it could mean disaster for everyone if I get it wrong. The risk is worth it. We're up against a wall and you know it."

Leaning against the table, he scowled. I waited, allowing him to mull it over. We'd had too many arguments lately and the stress was not worth it if it fractured the last shred of friendship we had after that kiss.

Finally, he looked at me.

"The Chimera are watching the World's End," he said. "We saw it on patrol. Even if what you're looking for is there, getting past them will be tricky. A simple illusion won't work and too much Colour will draw their attention."

"We'll figure it out once we scout the area," I countered. "The only way to know is to see it."

"We'll have to go past midnight to avoid the crowds. And if you phase, the Chimera will know we're around."

"So, is that a yes?"

His brow creased. "A reluctant one."

"I'll find you at midnight," I told him. "Oh, and make sure you're alone when I pop in."

Rory cringed and nodded. "Aye, I won't make that mistake again."

Leaving him to his clean up, I lingered in the tunnel, my thoughts troubled. Vanora was in love with Rory and he'd let her kiss him the night I came back to the Warren. No wonder she disliked me. Rory was — I shook my head.

Romance was more trouble than it was worth.

15

Edinburgh wasn't exactly a sleepy city. Even after midnight, people still walked around the Royal Mile, though three quarters of them were blind drunk.

Rory stood beside me, studying the World's End. Thankfully he'd been alone when I'd phased into his room, though Ignis had yowled in protest when I'd asked him to stay behind.

Why were all the men in my life so difficult? I made a mental note to thank Jaimie for being so uncomplicated the next time I saw him.

We huddled in the shadow of a doorway, nestled back off the footpath. I didn't know what I was looking for, and the sight that greeted us was exactly the same as it had been in broad daylight.

Whoever or whatever Yenris'del was, it wasn't here…or I was too stupid to see it.

The close behind the pub was shrouded in

darkness and the moment I focused on its depths, it began to distort and elongate. I sighed as the end stretched into infinity. It reminded me of the infinite reflections a mirror cast when it reflected another. It just got smaller and smaller until it was too far away to see any farther.

"I don't like this," Rory muttered, squinting at the dark close. "I can't see anything, let alone sense the supernatural. All this is doing is giving me a complex." He tapped his temple. "All the shortcomings of the Druids are on display right now. This is why we've never been able to fight back. We can't see the enemy."

I didn't take my eyes off the close as I punched him on the arm. "Until now."

"You really need to stop punching me. You're stronger than you look." He rubbed his arm. "What can you see?"

I squinted, trying to focus on the illusion. "It's doing that weird stretching thing again. The close with no end."

"I could walk in there—"

"And they'd see you," I interrupted. "Besides, I'm pretty sure that illusion is a trap in itself."

"Humans walk in there all the time," Rory stated.

"But they're not supernaturals."

"Hmm…a Druid honey pot."

I glared at him and shook my head. "Can we leave the crass jokes for another time?"

"You're the one who took it there," the Druid retorted. "It also means something that's enticing."

"Stop it." I punched him in the arm again. "I'm trying to think."

"Can you phase past it?" Rory asked.

I squinted at the close and frowned. "No. The illusion is stopping me."

"Maybe we should walk around the block and see if we can find another way through."

I leaned back against the door. I felt useless, despite the power I had at my disposal. I was missing something…

"Yenris'del lingers at the World's End," I murmured. "*Yenris'del*. Where are you?"

A presence lingered at my side in the darkness and a shiver ran down my spine. My senses screamed at me and I turned my head to the side, afraid of what I'd find.

A petite woman stood in the shadows beside me like she'd been there the whole time. Where she'd come from was a complete mystery. I hadn't seen or heard anything, and the door behind us hadn't opened, otherwise I would have fallen flat on my backside.

A sharp bolt of familiarity struck me as our gazes met. Her feline features were older and her golden curls were streaked with silver, but it was definitely the same woman.

"*You*," I whispered.

Rory jumped and cursed in Gaelic at the sight of the small woman. "Where did she come from?"

I shook my head in bewilderment and held his hand to quieten him. "I know you. You helped my father and I escape."

The Fae pressed her finger to her lips, a finger that was tipped with a pointed nail, then glared at Rory.

"He's with me," I told her. "No exceptions."

"I hope this is the infamous Yenris'del," he said, narrowing his eyes at the Fae. "Because I so knew you were a person."

She pressed her finger to her lips again and snatched my hand. I had a second to grab Rory before we phased.

We landed in the blink of an eye, and I breathed deeply as I looked around the unfamiliar living room. I didn't know what I was expecting, but it wasn't a couch, coffee table, and television. The overhead electric light was on, bathing the room in a warm glow.

"*O mo chreach*," Rory exclaimed, clutching my hand so tight I thought my bones were going to break under the pressure.

"What are you doing here?" I asked Yenris'del. "I saw you in my father's visions."

"This world is exhausting," she said, not listening to me. "It's too far away from home."

The phase seemed to exhaust her, and I placed my hand on her shoulder. "Then why did you come?"

"Edinburgh radiates with energy. It's better than nowhere," she glared at Rory, "apart from you."

Bewildered, he stared at her. "Me?"

"Greedy Druids," she said, slapping Rory on the back of the head. "Taking a place of power all for yourselves."

"*Ow*," he cried. "I don't know what you're talking about."

"I think she means the volcano," I said.

"What about it? It's extinct."

"She feels it," the Fae said, waggling a finger at me. "You are not the only beings who feed off nature, *boy*."

"We don't feed on anything," he fired back. "We *nurture*, not take."

"It's because you're too far away from the portal in Ireland, isn't it?" I asked her.

"My kind were confined to the Isle long ago," she confirmed. "But places like this help us thrive. Humans claim they build cities where they are defensible or close to water or close to food, but in truth, everything holds a little magic."

"So, you're saying the Fae live in human cities because they're places of power?" Rory asked.

"You don't see us living in tents in the wilderness, do you?" Yenris'del snapped. "Stupid boy."

"Can you go back?" I asked her.

"Many of us cannot," she replied, hinting at what I suspected was her punishment for helping my father. "*Politics*."

I frowned. The Fae were refugees in a foreign world, much like the Druids.

"I know nothing of my Fae heritage," I told her. "Your politics…"

Yenris'del raked her gaze over me, clearly unimpressed by what she saw. "I can tell."

"I saw you in my dreams," I told her. "You called me. How?"

She nodded. "I am what our people call a Dreamweaver. That is my Fae magic. That of dreams."

"And mine?"

Yenris'del sighed and gestured for me to sit.

I perched on the edge of the couch as she sank down into a well-worn dip in the right-hand cushion. Rory chose to stand, his palm lingering on the hilt of his knife in clear warning.

"Your blood makes your power extraordinary," she said, eyeing the Druid. "Without the other, you'd just be a plain Fae with no talent or…" she sneered at Rory, "a mediocre Druid."

If what Yenris'del was saying was true, then the only reason I could Spirit Walk or phase or summon negative energy was because I was of mixed blood. If I wasn't, then I'd be a regular Fae or Druid. But that didn't sound so bad to me.

"Excuse me," Rory exclaimed. "*I have talent.*"

I rolled my eyes. "Neither seems mediocre after living most of my life as a human."

"*Pfft.*" She threw her hands into the air in disgust. "You know nothing."

"That's why I'm here. I have no one else to turn to. My father is gone and…"

Her gaze flickered to mine, though she seemed to already know about my dad. Perhaps the fact I was here at all was knowing enough.

"You've been taking souls," she said after a moment.

I froze. "Only in self-defence."

Yenris'del clucked her tongue. "Each soul you take chips away at your own. A little comes off here, a little comes of there, and sooner or later…"

"Sooner or later what?" Rory demanded.

She shrugged. "Who knows. No one has ever gotten that far."

I thought about the black goop and scowled. "How can negative energy—"

"It's not negative energy," she said with a roll of her eyes. "Don't you know anything?"

"Obviously not!" I exclaimed. "I never knew my Fae mother, did I? I thought I was human!"

"It's your manifestation of the fabric between life and death. It's the veil."

"The veil? But I became essence. I… I possessed Owen and took his truth. I changed a little girl's memories… How is that death?"

"You *become* the veil."

"What does that mean?" I pleaded. "I don't understand!"

"Life and death are the same," Yenris'del told me blandly. "Spirit here, spirit there. Spirit, soul… they are just words. Doesn't matter."

"I think I understand now," Rory murmured. "It's not death you control, Elspeth. It may feel like it, but it's not. Death is just a word for the transcendence of spirit from the flesh."

"Finally, he shows some intelligence," Yenris'del muttered. "Death is just another world—one we all must travel to. Flesh is finite."

I blinked, the pieces falling into place. "I control people's spirits and the forces which take them to the next life…and bring them to new flesh. Souls… But they're the one thing no one is able to touch."

"Supposedly," Yenris'del declared, as if she knew something no one else did. "They try. They fail. Sometimes they get it right, but not for long. *Foolish.*"

Maybe that explained the souls Delilah caught for her constructs and how Ignis came to be blurred. Someone, in some far away reality, had been messing with things that ought to have been left alone.

I shook my head. If I thought about it too much, my brain might explode before I figured it all out. What was important was our reality and the prophecy which loomed over my head.

"You are reckless." Yenris'del flicked my forehead, the fingertip stinging my skin. "You've been dragging Fae into the next world, body and soul, and upsetting *everything.*"

I pouted. "Well, they should stop trying to kill me then."

"What they do may not be right, but they want to go home just like your Druids do. They want to live."

"We didn't come here for an ethical debate," Rory snapped. "What do you want with Elspeth?"

"Balance," Yenris'del snapped. "She must know what she is in order to preserve the separation between here and there. Otherwise, it will all come tumbling down."

I sucked in a sharp breath. "The dead could roam the Earth?"

"Spirits. Ghosts. Echoes," the Fae rattled off. "If there's in-between, there's no path to the next life. If you want to send a soul across the veil, then you must leave their flesh behind." That's why I saw those echoes last night, though now I realise they weren't remnants.

"I saw them," I said. "But…where are they?"

"In a place you made for them, knowing or not," she replied. "Given enough power, they will break out and tear the veil. Then there will be problems."

"How is she supposed to separate souls from their bodies?" Rory asked with a scowl. "Tell her that, because all you've done so far is scare her."

"Her ability is the rarest of them all," Yenris'del snapped, rising from the couch. "There is no instruction manual I can give you. Now that she understands the consequences, she can learn how to separate. Her ability is instinctual. It comes from her soul. *She knows.*"

Yenris'del's words sank into my mind, even though they weren't directed at me. *She knows.* It was a simple statement, but it explained a great deal. I had a knowing that awoke with my father's death. I seemed to have a natural talent for the supernatural…and when I'd stood on the train platform the day after the battle in Calton Cemetery, I'd suddenly understood all the nasty things Vanora had said to me in Gaelic. It was a *knowing* that came with the strange Fae ability linked to my deepest self.

Was my soul the skeleton key of all souls? If so, it just gave a whole new edge to the prophecy.

"So, I can control the veil and the passage of souls," I said. "I can force them one way or another, but the voices—"

"It is a dark power," Yenris'del said. "It will seduce you if you let it."

"Or others force you to it," Rory drawled, referring to the Chimera.

"Yenris'del," I began. There was one thing I wanted to ask above all else but hadn't had the courage after all the things she'd already dumped on me. "My mother. I know you helped my father but did you… Did you know her?"

"You have something she never had," Yenris'del replied, not answering the question.

"You can walk into death," Rory murmured, his expression falling.

"And across worlds," the Fae added. "Now that you have returned, war will come with you at its centre. It has already begun to stir."

"The prophecy," I murmured. "What do you know about it?"

She grasped my arm and pulled me close. "Druid or Fae," she hissed, her claws bit through the fabric of my jumper and dug into my skin. "Your destiny is to choose, but not all choices are clear."

"*Let her go*," Rory snarled, shoving her away from me.

Yenris'del's gaze snapped to the Druid and her expression twisted. "She is not yours to love, Druid. She is not destined for the likes of you."

I rose and tugged at his sleeve. "Rory…"

He nodded and broke away from the Fae. Something had changed in her.

"You can't come back here," Yenris'del rasped. "We've already spoken too long." She rushed towards me, her eyes wild. "*Get out!*"

What came next happened so fast, I barely had time to blink. Rory lunged towards the Fae, drawing his knife as an unfamiliar power rose in the little apartment.

Panicking, I grasped his arm and phased.

16

Rory and I landed on the Royal Mile.

He leaned against the window of a closed shop and pressed his forehead against the cool glass. Phasing still made him nauseous, it seemed.

I stood beside him, my gaze moving from window to window, wondering if any of them housed Yenris'del's tiny apartment. Sighing, I made sure our illusion was in place.

"Do you believe what she said?" Rory asked, turning his head so he could look at me.

"It's hard to believe anything in this world," I replied. "Magic has its boundaries, but it's still pretty fantastical. Controlling the flow of souls into death? Sure, but knowing that black stuff is the veil between life and the hereafter…"

Perhaps I hadn't erased Owen's soul after all, just merely given him an express pass to the next life where he'd begin anew with no memory of his life before. I shivered, wishing I'd brought a jacket, even though it was the middle of summer—Scotland was still cold at midnight, though.

"I thought the shadow was someone else living inside me and I was just a conduit," I continued. "Now I understand that it was me this entire time. I inherited my mother's curse. The Chimera couldn't have her, and now they're trying to turn me in her place." She didn't matter anymore; I was the bigger prize.

"At least we know." He pushed off the window and frowned. "Even though Goldilocks was off her head."

I gathered he meant crazy and shrugged. Everything was a little bonkers in this world, though I knew Yenris'del wasn't entirely herself because she wasn't in the right reality and her connection to it was weak at best. Besides, she hadn't told me anything I didn't already know or suspect, but at least I understood it now, and when someone understood something fully, they could make better choices.

"If what Yenris'del said was true, then the prophecy is more deadly than we thought," I said. "I could send a whole legion of souls across the veil without even blinking. A click of the fingers…" I sighed. "The only thing that's saved us is the fact that I haven't figured out how yet."

I didn't want to admit it to myself, let alone think the words, but I was… I was extinction.

I could call myself half-Fae, half-Druid,

supernatural, a warrior—*a sheòid*—or a *bò bhrònach* all I wanted. All those things made me who I was, but my purpose for being in this world was to remake it—to remove one of two supernatural races from existence. It was prophesied.

Born of ashes, dead in darkness, a soul who bridges the gap has the power to destroy Druid and Fae alike. When the black sun rises, death will choose the hand of fate.

It wasn't all bad, though. It seemed the foretelling only extended to the Druids or the Fae…for now.

Suddenly, the fantasy I'd had about life after all this dissolved and I thought about my mother. She was a full-blooded Fae and the ramifications of her power—the power she'd passed to me—was too great to comprehend. Perhaps her death, before the Chimera could turn her, was a blessing in disguise.

I hated myself for even thinking it and pushed her hazy memory away.

"I understand what I am now," I said to Rory. "Do you?"

He nodded, his expression grave. "I won't let you go through this alone, Elspeth."

She is not yours to love, Druid. She is not destined for the likes of you.

I shook my head. "How do I kill the monsters without becoming one myself? I could never live with myself if I hurt you, Rory, though I seem to be doing that already."

"Ach, I've got a rune over my heart, remember?" he stated. "Besides, it isn't exactly the apocalypse."

My cheeks heated. "Isn't it? It would be for the Fae. A whole world, erased just because I willed it."

"But you have a choice."

"What about the prophecy?"

"What about it?" he asked. "I thought you were going to destroy it. You do realise that it doesn't specifically say you have to choose one or the other… or choose at all. That's just a conclusion everyone's jumped to. You get to choose the hand of fate, Elspeth."

We could have debated the English language all night, but I was beginning to feel exposed lingering on the street.

"Let's go back," I said to Rory, shivering as a cool breeze rose. "We've hung around here too long."

"Do you want to phase?" he asked. "Because I need some advanced warning. My stomach lining is never going to be the same."

I hesitated. What if using my Fae powers was adding to the trouble I was causing with the veil? If I tore a hole in it, there was no telling what could come out of it and into the world of the living. Just because I hadn't seen anything in death didn't mean there wasn't any malicious souls waiting to take advantage of my stupidity.

"We can use the portals," Rory told me, "but they won't open until morning."

I blinked and glanced up at him. "Morning?"

"Because of the whole Chimera lockdown thing,"

he replied with a frown. "That Yenris'del has you rattled, doesn't she?"

I nodded. "Yeah."

Rory cracked his knuckles. "Well, either way, we're going to have to face the music with the Elders. They're going to want to hear about what we learned, you know."

"Sorry," I muttered. "I didn't think it was going to be that enlightening."

He grimaced. "I agreed to come with you while on a good behaviour bond, so I'm equal parts at fault."

I sighed. There I went breaking all the rules again. Shor was going to blow a fuse when we showed up in the morning.

"What's the time?" I wondered.

"About half one, my guess," Rory said, squinting at the sky. For once, the stars were shining overhead, barely visible through the light pollution of the city. "We have about four and a half hours."

"*Four and a half hours?*"

"I could try to open one, but after the hellhound incident, I think I better not. Besides, the Elders put up a ward around the Warren. They can't block Fae abilities, though."

I narrowed my eyes, annoyed at myself. All the progress I'd made with my confidence had begun to unravel the moment Yenris'del popped my bubble of obliviousness.

Instead, I grabbed Rory's arm and began to walk up the Mile. "Let's walk a while."

"Bold move, considering the climate."

I didn't like being outside any more than he did, but if the veil was that fragile…

We'd hardly gone a block before I sensed trouble. Rory felt it too, as his whole body tensed.

Ahead, a woman walked towards us along the Mile, her hands thrust deep into the pockets of her jacket. She was ordinary to look at—tall, medium weight, long mousey hair, soft features, and sharp eyes—so I hesitated at first, not sure if she was or wasn't the source of my uneasiness. It wasn't outside the realm of possibility that she was just walking home from a night out. *But…* There was always a but in this new world I found myself a part of.

As her gaze met mine and my illusion slipped, the first thought that came to mind was, *I didn't know there were female Chimera.*

Her lips curved into a triumphant smile that said, *gotcha.*

"So…" I began.

"How's your endurance training going?" Rory muttered.

"Wh—" I didn't have time to finish before he'd grabbed my hand and pulled me to the right, the sudden jerk almost gave me whiplash.

Our boots beat out a furious rhythm as we sprinted down Cockburn Street, the steep decline making our flight almost uncontrollable. Luckily, there was no traffic because we cut through the roundabout at the bottom, heading straight across the middle.

Hurtling down a flight of stone stairs, we found ourselves in a green garden area by the Waverley train station. Rory led the way, his knowledge of the hidden corners of Edinburgh kept us one step ahead of the Fae perusing us.

He doubled back and we ran up another set of stairs, emerging onto another road. Rory grabbed my hand and we sprinted across the street, narrowly avoiding a bus.

Dashing down a pedestrian walkway, we passed an impressive stone building. Banners hung between the Greek columns, declaring it as the Scottish National Gallery. There was no one around to see us run, other than a lonely security guard who walked through the courtyard, but we were hidden from him in any case.

We wove through some bollards, darted in-between the gallery and another building—likely another museum—across another road, and down into what I recognised as the Princes Street Gardens.

I hadn't dared to look back even once, but as we slipped into the shadows of the greenery, I chanced it. The Chimera emerged at the top of the stairs, her darkened form backlit by the orange street lights. She looked like a demon delighting in the hunt as she scanned the path below, unaffected by the desperate chase.

Rory urged me onwards and we snuck through the gardens. Above, I could see the castle on the hill, towering over everything like a symbol of solidarity for the besieged—if that was even a thing.

I heaved in laboured breaths, knowing I'd only gotten this far because of Darby's borderline torture sessions in the Druid's mediocre gym. Sweat beaded across my forehead and ran down my spine, and I wanted nothing more than to collapse right where I stood.

I pressed my back against a tree and shook. This was my life now. Running. Fear. The one thing standing between life and death. How could I continue, knowing I was destined to kill so many?

Rory grasped my shoulders and shook me out of my daze.

"We can't go any farther," he whispered. "We have to fight."

I shook my head, my lungs burning.

"Elspeth, you can't be afraid. *Who* you are has nothing to do with *what* you are."

"What if I make things worse?"

"There are Chimera on our tail right now, and they won't let up until they capture us both. It's us or them. If you won't phase… We can't lead them back to the Warren."

"Hiding behind a tree like a pair of wide-eyed rabbits," a voice crooned from the darkness. "Do yourself the honour of facing your fate in the light, Druid."

Rory pulled out his knife and held it at the ready —fingers tight around the handle and the blade facing downward. He took a deep breath, then stepped out of the shadow of the tree.

I followed, my heart still beating wildly, but at least my breath had begun to catch up.

The woman stood on the lawn, unarmed, though I could sense her latent power—and she had a great deal of it. The shite was about to hit the fan and I wasn't sure who was about to splatter.

"Running is futile," she said with a grin. "We will catch you eventually."

"Like hell you will," Rory snarled.

"The time of the Chimera is upon you, Druid. The black sun stands next to you, ready to rise. Can't you feel it?" Her gaze moved to mine and she held out her hand. "Come with me, Elspeth, and you will never be weak again. *Come home.*"

"Home?" I scoffed. "Your world is not my home. *This one is.*"

"I won't ask again."

"Then save your breath, because my answer will always be the same."

"*Then I will make you.*" The Chimera cried out in rage and came at us with terrifying speed.

Rory reacted like a bolt of lightning, his Colour splintering in sharp crystal prisms around his hand and along his blade. He struck, the knife plunging into her shoulder, and they landed in a heap on the grass.

The Fae let out a shriek so powerful it stabbed my eardrums and I clapped my hands over my ears. If it wasn't for our combined illusions, all of Edinburgh would have heard it.

"Elspeth!" Rory shouted as his Colour held the woman down.

I lunged, forcing myself out of the fog that clung to my mind, and shoved Rory off the Fae. My hands grasped her head and I called on the Darkness lingering under the surface of my Colour…and didn't hold back.

The warmth faded from my skin and turned blue, the black essence of the veil oozing from my fingers. The substance bled into the Chimera's hair and smeared over her skin, sucking the life from her physical form.

Separate the soul from the body…

"You need to stop hunting me," I hissed, my voice not entirely my own. "You will never twist me to your cause."

"It's already too late," the woman managed to choke out. "You will go. *You—*"

Whatever she was going to say next was cut off abruptly as her body began to crumble from the inside out. Her features froze and cracked, then turned to ash in my hands as I tore her soul from her living body and fed it through the veil. Instinct drove me, the knowledge I felt in my soul guided the Fae into the mist of death.

I hardly understood what was happening as an icy breeze swept around me like an invisible tornado. My hair buffeted in all directions and the ash swept across the gardens like a dust storm in the middle of the desert.

And as soon as it had begun, it was over.

My palms hit the grass and I stared at the place the Chimera had lay, numb and wide-eyed. Rory's knife fell, landing with a dull thud.

The air settled and the warmth of the summer evening started to heat my skin as the veil retreated.

"Elspeth?" Rory's voice was barely a whisper. "The others are coming. They're not far…"

I killed her. I didn't feel anything after what I'd done to all those other Chimera but understanding brought a whole new set of ethics I hadn't bargained for.

I'd killed people. Human, Druid, Fae…it was all the same. A life was a life.

Why did it bother me now? *Because you only ever killed once before.* Owen. *And you liked giving him what he deserved.*

In that moment, I wished I was nothing more than a plain, ordinary Druid. A natural pacifist.

"*Elspeth.*" Rory dragged me to my feet, his eyes wild. "This isn't the time to check out. There'll be Chimera all over this park in thirty seconds." He shook me into coherency. "You have to phase us into the Warren. *Now.*"

Low whistles echoed through the night, one answering the other in a wave that spread in all directions. They were coming.

I didn't think about it. I grabbed Rory's hand and

we disappeared in the blink of an eye and landed in a heap at the foot of *Salle*, both of us gasping for breath.

Vanora appeared out of nowhere and kicked Rory in the ribs. "Where in the hell have you been?"

It was then I realised the Warren was in complete uproar. Leaves littered the cavern floor, as did chunks of crystal that had broken away from the ceiling. Druids sat amongst the twisting roots of the willow, some crying and others clutching their heads.

Rory scrambled to his feet and I did the same, both of us trying to make sense of what was going on.

"Galavanting around the city with things the way they are," Vanora snarled at us. "How dare you put us in danger like this! We needed you and you were gone!"

Rory grasped her arm, forcing the Druidess to look at him. "Vanora, *what's going on?*"

Her eyes were cool, but her words felt like a white-hot poker stabbing into my chest. "The Elders have been taken."

17

———

Vanora's words sliced into me like a knife.

"What do you mean, the Elders were taken?" I asked, edging between her and Rory before they could come to blows—not that I was any safer.

"Everyone was asleep and then the whole Warren began to shake," she said with narrowed eyes. "It wasn't until the tremors subsided that we realised they were missing."

"A distraction," Rory murmured.

I shook my head. "How did they get in?"

"I have no idea," Vanora raged. "One minute the Warren was calm and the next, it felt like the whole place was going to come down on our heads. Osna was struck by a piece of crystal from the ceiling!"

"Osna?" My head turned towards the Druidess. "Is she okay?"

"Ach, she'll be fine, but not if we can't do

something about this. The whole Warren is compromised."

"We have to figure out how they got in and plug the hole," I said. "But I don't know how…"

"Some of the older Druids may know," Rory told me. "It's a little out of my depth, too. Prism building is another one of those tricky skills."

"Ach, there you are." Jaimie strode towards us, his hair and beard dusted with a fine layer of crystal dust. He sparkled as he moved, which was a total juxtaposition. "What in the world is going on?"

I glanced at Rory. It didn't seem like the best time to keep things to ourselves, considering the fact that I suspected this was all linked. I told the Druids everything.

They stared at me wide-eyed as the tale unfolded —my dreams and how the Chimera were attempting to infiltrate them, Yenris'del and her revelations about my powers, and the fight we'd just had in the Princes Street Gardens.

"It was your dreams," Vanora stated, glaring at me. "They used the Fae Dreamweaver's sloppiness to get to the Elders. *If* she was sloppy and not a double agent."

Maybe she was right. If Yenris'del could contact me through my dreams while I was inside the Warren, then nothing was stopping anyone else doing the same to the Elders—apart from their lack of Fae blood— but maybe I was the link which allowed the jump.

"Yenris'del a double agent?" I blinked.

"She was a little loopy," Rory said.

"Yeah, because she's cut off from her world since she helped my father escape the Chimera. *She's starving.*"

Vanora snorted. "And would likely do anything to get back to her world."

"Then why would she help me?" I asked. Perhaps I was too trusting. Twenty years was a long time, and anyone could change irrevocably after what Yenris'del had been through.

Rory sighed. "It seems she's not without heart."

"It doesn't help with the Elders," Vanora declared. "They're still gone, and we're still open to attack."

"This is an attempt to draw you out," Jaimie said after some careful consideration.

"Of course, it is!" I cried. "That doesn't mean we shouldn't do anything!"

"They're the most powerful of us," Vanora said, her eyes wide. "If the Chimera can control them, there's nothing stopping the rest of us to follow suit."

"It's only speculation," I told her. "There's no evidence they were possessed."

"Unless they went willingly," Rory murmured, glancing at me.

"Why would they?" Vanora demanded. "They'd never——"

"Because she's the alpha," Jaimie stated, looking at me. "That hell wolf saw it and so did the Chimera. This is the moment we've been training for."

"Strike them in the heart," Vanora declared. "Kill them once and for all."

"This isn't about killing anyone!" I exclaimed, the fears I'd had in the gardens rushing to the surface. "It's about getting the Elders back in one piece. Delilah is my grandmother. She…she's the only family I have left. Without them, we're lost. Do you think I can lead just because some wolf from a world that smells like a rotten fart thinks I'm the alpha? *Because I can't.* I don't know what you want me to do! If I make one wrong move, I could tear the veil between life and death, then the Chimera will be the least of our problems."

Everyone fell silent, even the injured and confused Druids who lingered in the cavern.

"Elspeth," Rory began, but I didn't want to hear it.

"I'm forever causing you problems," I told them. "It's me they want. I should go and end this. If I wasn't here—"

"You tried that, lass, and it didn't work." Jaimie said. "We're in this together. It's no one's fault. It's just the way the world is."

"We'll find the Elders," Vanora said, her frown deepening. "Us four…and your cat if he'll come."

"We won't let you face this alone, Elspeth," Rory told me. "*Tha sinn còmhla riut.*" *We are with you.*

I froze as the Druids stared at me like I was their leader, like I had all the answers. No one had ever looked at me like that before. *Plain, ordinary Elspeth*

Quarrie. A lifetime of conditioning wasn't easily undone.

Glancing at *Salle*, my arms throbbed with phantom pain from the prisms that'd bound me all those months ago. *How far I'd come*. Even death was no match for me.

That's it. Death!

I'd find some answers in the grey lands beyond the veil. That's where the Chimera knew I'd go, just like I did to verify Yenris'del's message. They understood my mother's power enough to covet her, and they knew me by extension. Well, enough to anticipate what I'd do, which meant I'd have to be equally as tricky to outsmart them.

In other words, the proverbial ransom note would be waiting for me beyond the veil, but it'd be boobytrapped somewhere along the way. Jaimie was right about that.

I shook my head, snapping myself out of my daze, and glanced at Rory.

"Elspeth, are you sure?" he asked.

I didn't reply. I merely called on my power and began dissolve into the essence that would pass me into a world that was made only of sprit.

"Where is she going?" Vanora demanded, her voice fading as I passed through the veil.

The colour bled from the Warren as I stepped into the mist, then the caves disappeared completely. They sat out of space and time, thus didn't exist in death. It was a place even the spirits couldn't reach. Perhaps

Vanora was right after all. The Chimera had used Yenris'del's link to my dreams to get to the Elders. I was their only way in.

Guilt shuddered through me as I walked. My lack of knowledge about the Fae had brought the enemy into the one place they were not permitted to go. This was all my fault, just like everything else that'd gone wrong in this world.

It wasn't until I was in the city that I realised I'd crossed without any protective runes. Well, it was too late for that now.

I couldn't be afraid of what I was anymore. An entire race of people were counting on me to prevail. If I lost my wits now, the aftershock would be terrible.

I just had to be okay with it.

A formless wind stirred up around me, swirling the mists and driving them into long ribbons.

Currents, I thought. *Those are the invisible roads souls take. It has to be.*

I peered into the grey world around me, my eyes widening as I began to see what the mists had been hiding—ghosts, spirits…*souls.*

They swept past me in waves, some crying out, others silent, some were even stuck in their state of death. Each one ebbed and flowed on the currents, going their separate ways.

Every so often a spirit would peel away from the mist and regain human form, before running off into the grey. Where they were going, I had no idea. Back to life to haunt the living? Perhaps.

It was then that I realised the runes had been protecting me, but for the wrong reasons. I couldn't see the spirits who'd been crying out to me. I couldn't sense the currents that took souls to the next life; I couldn't detect the lost and malevolent. *I'd been blind.*

Death wasn't empty. Death was full of life in transition.

My eyes were open and what I saw changed *everything*. The prophecy still hung over my head, but I no longer feared what I could do. I had control over it and I could choose the path a soul took…or leave it to nature to decide. There was no reason for me to be everyone's judge, jury, and executioner. I wasn't death. I was merely the bridge between worlds.

The currents of death, the veil, the passage of these souls…I could control them all, but I didn't want to enslave anyone. Thinking about Ignis, I pressed the heel of my palm against my chest. The cat helped me of his own free will. *Perhaps…*

"Hello?" I murmured. "Is anyone out there?"

The currents continued to flow, undisturbed by a strange woman visiting from life.

"If there's anyone out there, any spirit, you don't have to be afraid of me. I'm not here to disturb the natural order of things. I…" I took a deep breath, feeling a little silly for talking to dead people floating in a sea of primordial mist. Well, I supposed I'd done stranger things. "I am Elspeth Odhweine and I need help. If any Druids linger… If any spirits can show me how to help our Elders, please come forth. *Please.*"

A long moment passed before I felt the grey stir.

A woman emerged from the mist, her body taking shape as she approached. She was lithe and tiny, a delicate girl near to my age, though I knew it was just the way she wanted to present herself to me—long hair, soft cheekbones, intelligent eyes. *Innocent.*

Still, I hesitated. I had to be careful, lest something evil was hiding behind her mask.

The spirit held out her hand and waited. Taking a chance, I lifted my own and reached out to meet her halfway.

Our fingers brushed ever so slightly, and a shiver of recognition passed through me. My gaze met hers and I tilted my head to the side.

"Who are you?" I asked, my voice a whisper on the currents of death.

She merely smiled and threaded her fingers through mine, linking us together.

I wasn't afraid. Her presence was calming, and even a little warm in a place that had no colour or feeling.

She beckoned me to follow, tugging on my hand, and we passed through the currents. It was as if I was wading through waist-deep water as I felt the ghostly fingers of spirits passing by brush my legs. Until now, I had been unfeeling, but without the runes, my senses were expanding.

The spirit stopped in front of me and swatted her hand through the air. I gasped as the grey vista shimmered and images began to appear. They were blurry at first, but it wasn't long before I recognised what I was looking at.

Yenris'del struggling with sickness.

Yenris'del with the Chimera.

Yenris'del striking a deal.

Vanora was right. The Fae had an ulterior motive for drawing me out, but it wasn't all malicious. She still harboured some compassion for my father's plight, though she couldn't live with the absence of her world. She was wasting away and would become twisted like the creatures who plagued Ireland before the Witches opened their portal again.

Yenris'del was desperate…but weren't we all?

The spirit took my hand once more and led me though the vision. It dissolved like ink in water, swirling and clouding as our passage broke it apart.

There was no time to let it sink in, but there were more messages she wanted to tell me.

"The Elders?" I asked. "Do you know where they were taken?"

The spirit pressed her finger to her lips to silence me and nodded, her hair fluttering in the motionless wind.

I gathered she meant speaking of it was dangerous, even here, so I did as she wanted and remained tight-lipped.

We began to walk once more, floating on formless ground until the world began take shape around us. Life bled through the veil, thinning as the spirit nudged me towards the place I desperately wanted to see.

Grass sprung up underfoot and we climbed a steep incline, the star-studded sky stretching above. Rolling hills and mountains shimmered out of the haze, their dappled surfaces of rock, heather, and wild grasses stood out even in the dark of night.

We stood in the Highlands of Scotland, the spirit of the land strong enough to bring us close to its surface.

But it was morning outside. I hadn't been in death that long, had I? Maybe time flowed differently, or just appeared like the negative of an old film camera—all back to front.

The spirit pointed across the valley. Following her finger, I saw a thick copse of trees growing down the side of the dale and merging with the shore of a loch. It wasn't Loch Lomond, though how I knew was beyond me.

Wherever it was, the land was ancient…and powerful.

Squinting, I made out the shape of a series of jagged stones at the heel of the dale. They'd been fashioned into a haphazard circle, the rectangular rocks placed up on one end and pointing towards the sky.

I felt the spirit's unwavering certainty through our linked hands. This was where the Elders were being held.

Turning to her, I asked, "Who are you?"

The spirit smiled and pointed back the way we'd come.

"You were a Druid once, weren't you?"

She nodded and urged me back towards life.

"Thank you," I told her. "I won't let you down."

Her lips moved, forming a few solitary words—*I know you won't*—then the currents tugged her ghostly essence, dissolving her sprit back into the grey.

Not wanting to linger, I crossed the veil and emerged in the place where I'd entered. The Warren.

The Druids were arguing when I appeared, but my abrupt return had them turn towards me with dumbfounded expressions. I knew Spirit Walking wasn't that common, but it wasn't that weird, was it?

"See! I told you she'd come back," Rory declared, gesturing at me.

Vanora clearly didn't hold the same opinion. "You can't just disappear like that, Elspeth. Your cat showed up and nearly clawed my face off!"

Ignis, in his tabby cat shape, jumped out of *Salle's* branches and landed at my feet. He yowled and walked figure eights around my legs, furious that I'd gone wandering in death without him.

"I didn't know what else to do," I said, brushing away my embarrassment at being made the centre of attention once again. "A spirit came forth and showed me where the Elders were taken. A circle of stones in the Highlands."

"A stone circle?" Rory mused. "Those are Druid places…"

"Not on this Earth," Jaimie reminded him. "All kinds of people use henges, not just us."

"Henges?" I asked. "Like Stonehenge?"

"Aye," Rory replied. "Exactly like that."

Vanora wasn't having any of it. "And how do we know that's not a trap, too?" she demanded. "Henges have power of their own and if the Chimera have tapped into it, then who knows what will happen to us."

I glared at her. "We don't, but the spirit showed me the truth as she saw it. The Chimera are tricksters; it's in their blood. I can see that now."

"Then we just have to outsmart them," Jaimie declared. "We know how to use henges, too. I bet they don't know that."

I doubted it, but I didn't want to burst the shapeshifter's bubble. The Chimera had the Elders and it was still a mystery what the Chimera could do to them.

Vanora glanced at the Druids congregated around *Salle*. "What about the Warren? We can't just leave it undefended."

I followed her gaze and found Darby attending to an elderly Druid. She dabbed a damp cloth against his injured forehead with a grace and tenderness I never thought she would have possessed a few months ago. Now, I saw her differently.

"This place doesn't exist anywhere else but here," I told the others. "I couldn't even see it in death. No one can enter without passing through a portal of your making. The only reason I can phase in and out with my Fae abilities is because I'm half-Druid. My blood is the key, as it is yours."

"So the others are safe down here?" Jaimie asked.

I nodded. "It's the safest place in the entire world."

"You're different," Rory murmured. "What changed in the last half hour?"

"I've finally accepted who I am," I replied. "I have to be okay with what I can do. I can save them. I know I can."

He smiled and bowed his head. "Then we are at your command, *neach-gleidhidh*."

My cheeks heated and I punched him on the arm.

Vanora coughed, drawing my gaze to hers. She glared at me, her jealousy over my relationship with Rory clear for all to see.

"Can you take us to the stone circle?" Jaimie asked, as much to drive us to action as to break up the awkward love-triangle—even if it was a strictly one-way street I was desperately trying to get off.

I shrugged. "I've seen the place, but…"

"But?" Vanora demanded. "It's not the time for *buts*."

"I've never phased with more than one other person before," I told them. "Or gone that far. I mean, I've phased to places I haven't been to before, so that should be okay; but I don't know what will happen if we all go together. We might get dumped somewhere in-between." *Or land in a loch.*

"Every moment we stand here and doubt is a moment the danger the Elders face deepens," Vanora said, holding out her hand. "We go now or not at all."

"We're ready." Rory held out his too.

Ignis meowed, desperate not to be left behind again.

"Who's carrying the cat?" Jaimie asked.

Then, much to everyone's shock and amazement, Ignis began to alter his prisms. When he was done, kitten-Ignis clambered up my leg with his tiny sharp claws and fit into my jacket pocket.

"Avengers assemble," Rory said with a chuckle.

I rolled my eyes and grabbed their hands, Jaimie linking with them to make a circle.

Then, I phased.

18

———

The sun was rising when we appeared in the Highlands.

Jaime cursed as he let go of the others' hands and sat down on a rock. "My stomach lining shredded off," he complained, holding his gut. "How can you stand it, lass?"

"She doesn't feel anything," Rory told him with a chuckle.

Vanora didn't break a sweat, but I thought it might have been more pride than anything keeping her uncomfortableness from showing on her face.

"At least we made it in one jump," I said, pointing down the hillside.

The plateau the spirit guided me to jutted out from the craggy landscape, the canopy of the woods below brushed around its edges before it melted into the valley beyond. In the distance, the waters of the unknown loch glittered in the first rays of sun, but my gaze was drawn much nearer than that.

On the grassy outcropping, twelve upright stones had been placed meticulously in a circular pattern by peoples unknown. Some were tall, others were middling but seemed to follow a specific design. I sensed nothing Fae about the place, nor did I feel their presence. *Why did the spirit lead us here?*

I drew in a deep breath and gazed out over the valley. The beauty of the rugged highlands, paired with the ancient stones and flaming dawn, took my breath away. Never before had I sensed such a deep connection with a place or time as I did now.

But there was no sign of the Elders.

Rory gave me a worried look, then began to make his way down to the standing stones. The rest of us followed. Maybe answers were hidden within the henge.

The rays of the rising sun shone between the two largest stones, casting a long shadow across the henge as we approached.

"It's the Solstice," Vanora murmured. "The dawn of the longest day of the year."

Jaimie stood beside her. "I hope that's not an omen."

"So that's why the rocks are placed like that," I mused. "To mark celestial events."

"And to harness the powers of the Earth," Rory told me. "Everything is connected. Earth, sea, and sky." *Of course.* Thríbhís Mhór—the three spiralled triskele symbolising the Druidic homeland.

"Have you ever heard of Ley lines?" Vanora asked me.

I nodded. "It sounds familiar."

"It's a human term for the Earth energies which travel through the planet," she went on. "Humans and supernaturals built henges and other monoliths on places like these. But not all of them connect the right way, or at all."

"Does this one?"

She shrugged. "We're about to find out."

We picked our way down the rugged hillside and onto the plateau. Now that we stood at the edge of the henge, I was surprised to find it stood almost twice as tall as I did in some places.

The stones themselves sparkled with hints of its tumultuous creation—part glacial and part sediment from the ancient ocean—but it was also marked by hands unknown. Crescent moons, circles, arrows, curved serpents, and more adorned the jagged monoliths.

I traced the spirals and circles, wondering who had carved them. They'd been worn down by centuries—or perhaps millennia—of wind and rain, the once sharp edges blurred into the sedimentary stone.

"This place is old," Rory said. "These are early Pictish symbols."

"Pictish?" I asked, gazing at the marks.

"Ancient people," he replied. "They lived through the Highlands from the late Iron Age until the early Medieval period where they eventually became the first Gaelic Scots…or so human historians believe. It's difficult to know everything about a people without any written history."

I nodded. "Or when history is written by the winners."

"This isn't a history lesson," Vanora snapped. "We came here for the Elders and from what I can see, they're not here." Her glare turned to me.

"Don't look at me like that," I said. "I have no reason not to believe the spirit who showed me this place. She was a Druid once. We must be missing something."

"Who was she?" Jaimie asked. "Your spirit?"

I shrugged and looked to the stones. "I don't know. She could have been anyone, really. Death doesn't know the bounds of reality."

Ignis stirred inside my pocket and clawed his way out. He'd been so still, I'd almost forgotten he was there. It was highly likely he'd fallen asleep as per his usual nonchalance about all things Druid.

As he leapt, he grew into a full-sized tabby cat and began to prowl the edges of the henge. I watched him closely, noting his hesitation at walking through the stones.

"Ignis," I called, kneeling as the cat circled back towards me. "This is important." I smoothed back his silky fur. "Stay here and wait for us. If something happens, I know you'll sense it and do what you need to do. You were a warrior once, and you still are. Warriors know the importance of sacrifice in battle."

Ignis blinked up at me.

"Do you understand?"

He licked his whiskers and headbutted my knee. I gathered that meant yes.

"Elspeth," Jaimie said. "What do you know?"

"Ignis won't step inside the henge," I replied. "There's an illusion tied to it. There has to be."

"I can't sense anything," Vanora complained. "There's nothing here."

I walked around the circle, studying the symbols, measuring the distance between stones, but it wasn't until I stared into the rising sun of the Summer Solstice that I saw it.

The land swept away from me, lengthening into infinity. The dawn blurred, the burning pink and orange igniting the whole sky.

"Here," I declared, beckoning the others. "This is the way in."

"I can't see anything," Rory said, then he stilled. "This is exactly like the World's End, isn't it?"

I nodded. "Fae magic."

"A portal?" Jaime wondered.

"Fae can't open portals," Vanora told him.

"It's an illusion, not a portal," I said. "It's the way in—"

"To a trap," the Druidess interrupted.

"And the only way forwards," Rory declared. "This is where the battle begins."

"We vowed to face it together," Jaimie said, laying a hand on my shoulder. "*Tha sinn còmhla riut.*"

I took a deep breath as I looked back at the illusion between the stones. "Then we better get on with it."

Together, we passed through the monoliths and the sunrise blinked out, throwing us into complete darkness.

The ground disappeared from beneath my feet and we fell, but it wasn't far. The four of us landed in a heap on a cold, stony surface, Vanora cursing loudly and Rory grunting in pain. Luckily, Jaimie broke my fall, but he never complained about his landing.

"You okay, lass?" he murmured into my ear.

"I think so…"

"*Elspeth.*"

I looked up in shock at Delilah as she knelt beside me. "Delilah?"

"Yes, we are here." Her gaze took in the others, though she wasn't surprised to see us all together.

"Where are we?" I asked her.

"A cage," Rowen's voice came out of the murkiness.

"Somewhere underground." *Shor.*

"Well, the crew's all here," Vanora drawled, standing and dusting off her leggings.

I extracted myself from Jaimie's lap and looked around, realising we were in a cave. The walls were made of the same sedimentary rock as the henge, though it was more layered as if an ancient glacier had carved through the mountain range above. Likely, it'd created a natural crevasse that had eventually formed the caves where we were now imprisoned.

I still couldn't sense any magic, but that didn't mean there wasn't anything hiding in the shadows. The Fae had certainly had enough sense to give our little alcove some semblance of bars. They stretched across the length of the 'room', separating us from a larger cavern, though the rest disappeared into darkness.

Light was coming from somewhere, though there didn't seem to be a source I could pinpoint. *Illusions*. It was always illusions. They kept appearing like a bad smell I couldn't get rid of.

Blinking, I shook my head. "How did they even…?"

"The dreams," Delilah told me. "You were right to be wary of them."

"Told you so," Vanora stated, narrowing her eyes at me. "They took advantage of your ignorance."

"Stop rubbing it in, Vanora," Rory snapped. "We didn't know about it either, and we've had twenty-five years to figure it out."

I grasped Delilah's hands. "Did you… The others think you might have come willingly, but they tried to possess me in my dreams before. I—"

My grandmother smiled and shook her head. "That's not important now." I sensed the reverence in her tone and shied away. "Elspeth. Granddaughter. Now is the time. Do you understand?"

My heart lurched and I nodded. I wasn't ready. I had to be ready.

Jaimie shook the bars and grunted in frustration. "I can't feel my Colours."

Rory frowned and held out his hand. "Me either."

"None of us can access our Colour," Rowen told them. "Whatever this place is, they've warded it to neutralise us."

Vanora groaned and leaned against the cave wall. "This is the place where Druids go to get their powers stripped. *Perfect.*"

"*Not helping,*" Rory hissed.

"What?" she demanded. "The Chimera get their walking doomsday prophecy along with the six of us to open their monster portal to their evil lair. This whole thing was a trap to ensure their plans for world domination would succeed. We were stupid to think we could outsmart them."

"It's not over yet," I snarled, rising to my feet. "We haven't even begun."

"And what do you think you can do, huh?" the Druidess fired back. "You're the reason we're in here."

"What are you talking about?" Shor demanded.

Sighing, I told them how Rory and I had snuck out to find Yenris'del. Then all the bits where she had revealed the truth of my powers, her helping my father escape, her reality as an exile…and her treachery.

"She was right about that much at least," I added. "I can manipulate the veil and the currents on the other side. I hadn't truly seen death until a few hours ago and it made sense. I'd trapped those Chimera where they didn't belong, bodies and all, and they were trying to get out—almost like they were attempting to tear the veil."

"Your Spirit Walking interferes," Delilah mused.

A lightbulb blinked on inside my head, but Rowen spoke, stopping the idea from forming.

"That's all well and good," she said, "but for right now, the Chimera will come back to see if their trap caught Elspeth."

Shor turned to me. "Can you draw them all into death without the black sun rising?"

"I don't know. One soul at a time, yes. More than that? Who knows? They're going to have to let me out first, because I can't reach any of my powers, either."

"Then you have to convince them you're on their side," Rory said. "Trick the tricksters."

I scoffed, "That only worked with Owen because he was a gullible moron."

"That's because he was in love with you," the Druid retorted. "Jaimie and I saw it right before you—"

"*Raurich*," Delilah murmured, silencing him before he could go too far.

It always amused me how she used his full name,

though it sounded almost exactly the same as his shortened one, but I couldn't find it in me to even crack a smile.

"I highly doubt it," I said, rolling my eyes. The Fae had a strange way of showing it, but that's if Rory was right. "Somehow, I reckon his successor won't make the same mistake."

Trick the tricksters. It had merit, but I didn't know if I was that smart.

"They'll show up at some point," Jaimie said. "We have to make a plan. I'm not going to go down without a fight."

I closed my hands into fists and hesitated as a pulse vibrated through my fingers. Black goop began to colour my fingernails as the veil brushed up against me. I pushed it away before the others could see.

I could still feel my abilities, but not my Colour—whatever the Chimera had done to dampen the Druid also extended to me—but my Fae blood still churned unhindered. It was deliberate move on their part, it had to be. Now was not the time to throw caution to the wind.

"He comes," Rowen murmured, her eyes focused on the shadows.

I turned, my power flaring in warning at the unknown presence. A human shape peeled away from the darkness and I scowled at the man as he made himself known.

The Fae approached the bars, gliding like his feet didn't touch the ground. His illusion masked him as a strong, muscular man with angular, elf-like features. Long, inky black hair fell in a sleek, straight curtain around his shoulders—that I knew he didn't have to spend hours in front of a mirror with straighteners to achieve, though the image was amusing.

His clothes were strange—he wore a black, belted tunic and tight trousers, the former woven with scales of shiny obsidian-like metal. His boots came up to his knees and silver rings adorned his long fingers— fingers with pointed claw-tipped nails.

At first glance, his grace reminded me of an elf out of *Lord of the Rings*, but I knew the truth of what lurked underneath. He came from another world where fairytale nightmares were real.

"Elspeth Quarrie," he purred, looking me over like I was a shiny bauble. His eyes shone like silver, the irises almost metallic. "Finally, we meet face to face."

I grasped the bars, my power leeching into them.

"Well, you seem to know my name," I said with a sigh. "Care to tell me yours?"

"I am Mindel. The First of the Chimera of Earth."

The Fae smiled seductively, his power drawing me out of the confines of the cage. The cave lengthened behind him, just as the close behind the World's End had, and I bristled as everything came together.

I glanced back at the cell, and as Rory called out to me, his words were silent.

"They cannot hear us, if that is your concern," Mindel told me.

"It's not," I retorted, looking back at him. "What have you done with their magic?"

He waved his hand. "A little spell to keep them under control. You know how it is."

"No," I replied. "How is it?"

His gaze flickered to mine, his expression steely. "My, you *are* fiery. Just like your mother."

My snarl faded as my longing to know my mother pierced my heart.

Mindel smirked. "I understand you never got to meet her. A shame really. Now you stand before me, it's as if I'm seeing her born anew. It must have been a terrible burden for you father to have to look upon your face every day."

"Don't you dare bring my father into this," I raged. "You don't get to talk about him."

The Chimera clucked his tongue and shook his head back and forth ever so slowly. "You don't make the rules here, Elspeth."

"Neither do you."

He paused, waiting for me to elaborate.

"Your king pulls your strings, just as he did Owen's. You're nothing but a puppet."

"My king? Oh, do tell me more."

"Your king is not my master," I hissed. "I answer to no one."

His lips curved into a malicious smile. "Oh, but you do, Elspeth. You answer to your precious Elders."

"Caring is not answering to a higher power."

"Caring doesn't matter. We all answer to a higher

power, regardless of what we hold in life. Do you know of what I speak?"

My expression faded. "Death."

Mindel's lips curved upwards, the malicious smile twisting his otherwise perfect features. His power drew me closer before he spoke, and when he did, I felt terror like never before.

"*Born of ashes, dead in darkness, a soul who bridges the gap has the power to destroy Druid and Fae alike. When the black sun rises, death will choose the hand of fate.*"

My blood ran cold as he made me stand before him. "You want me to fulfil the prophecy right now, don't you?"

Mindel grinned and clapped his hands together. "And so it begins!"

This was it. This was the last stand of the Druids. If I'd known it was going to be here and now, I would have... *Would have what?* There was no preparing for this. The fan was spinning, and the proverbial poop was about to splatter. Extinction was upon us, *but I had the power to choose.*

Rory had to be right. The prophecy didn't say it had to be one or the other. I could still rewrite destiny.

"The black sun isn't rising today, Mindel," I snarled. "Nor will it ever."

"You dare challenge the sacred words of our people?" His illusion wavered and for a split second, his true face showed through. A ruined, twisted beast snarled, his magic the only thing keeping his flesh together. What kind of monster was this?

"I may have Fae blood, but you were *never my people*. Challenge me at your peril, Mindel. Your illusion is the only thing keeping you together… literally. I'd hate to see you *fall apart*."

"I will not make the same mistake my predecessor did," the Chimera snarled. "There will be no underestimating the power of the *Liash li Ashli*. Your threats are meaningless!"

He raised his hand and made a tight fist, and as his fingers curled, an invisible energy took hold of me and my knees buckled as my windpipe closed in on itself.

"You will bend to our will, Elspeth, *Liash li Ashli*," he said as I gasped for air. "You are not absolute. You are a pawn in a game much larger than any of us. This reality will be remade, and when we return to our world with the magic of your father's people, they—"

Mindel's speech was cut off as a flash of Colour tore through the cavern and hurled itself at his face. Ignis yowled as he shifted into his tiger shape and sunk his claws into the Chimera, cutting off the force crushing my throat.

I fell to my knees with a gasp as cool oxygen flooded my lungs and a popping sound echoed though the cave. A moment later, the Druids were at my back, helping me to my feet as Ignis enthusiastically mauled his prey.

"Elspeth," Rory said behind me, "now would be the time to call on some of that bad-assery we all know you have inside you."

"Then you better stand back," I warned, stretching out my hands.

As Mindel screeched, I called on the veil…and hoped to all that was good in the world that the black sun wouldn't rise with it.

19

As I called on the afterlife, my fingers turned black as I trailed them through the veil separating the living from the dead.

Mindel thrashed underneath Ignis's crushing weight, the tiger holding the Fae in place.

"Ignis." I gestured for him to stand aside.

The cat lifted his head, his blue stripes shimmering with prisms. When he saw my changing form, he stepped away and prowled to my side.

Mindel looked up at me and hissed, his torn flesh oozing red blood. I almost expected it to be black to match his heart.

I reached towards him, the veil dripping from my fingers like thick tar.

He muttered under his breath and slapped his palms onto the ground, sending a soundless shockwave through the rock. An answer came almost immediately. Thunder rolled through the cave, the reverberating sound shaking the earth.

"What in the world is that?" Rory murmured, standing beside me.

I already knew the answer. My blood sang at the presence of my own kind, but it was a tune only I could hear.

"Chimera," I said, knowing I didn't look much different in that moment.

Vanora hissed, "How many?"

I glanced at her, my vision hazy through their black veil. "*All of them.*"

Mindel began to laugh, his illusion flickering as he clutched his side. His teeth were stained red with blood and he spat at my feet. "You have no idea what you're doing, *Liash li Ashli*. You may walk in death, but you can still die."

I let the veil wrap around my hands and the chill of death spread across my skin, drawing all the colour from my flesh. "All things have an end, Mindel, but I doubt you thought this was going to be yours. You wanted this to be the final battle for Earth…" My lips curved into a wicked smile as the shadow of my darker self came forth. "*So, let's find out who wins.*"

"Druids, the time has come," Delilah said.

The Elders held out their hands, palms up, and together, they called on their Colours. Blue light filled the cavern as a glittering web of sharp angles and curves grew across the ceiling like crystal. It illuminated even the darkest crevasses, and for the first time since falling into the hole, we could see.

We stood in an enormous cave at least five times the size of the crystal cave that housed *Salle*. The ceiling dripped with banded stalactites, though the walls and ground were smooth enough from the thousands of years being worn down by one of the many glaciers that once carved through the Highlands. Openings dotted the vast expanse, leading to well-worn paths.

I felt the remnants of an illusion in the air and realised that this was the Chimera's base of operations on Earth. We'd fallen into the heart of the hornet's nest.

It wasn't supposed to go like this.

Mindel was right. I had no idea what I was doing.

Chimera swarmed out of the tunnels, their blades glinting in the cool light of the Elder's prism. There had to be at least a hundred of them. A hundred against seven…and a tiger.

Rory, Vanora, and Jaimie stood before the Elders, shielding them. They drew their knives, but compared to the swords the Chimera held, they were no match.

They are going to die, the shadowy voice whispered into my ear. *Unless you let me go. I can take them all away…*

"Elspeth?" Rory called as the Chimera formed a line before us.

Mindel rose, his silver eyes glinting in the blue light of the prism. Nothing stood between us, not unless the Elders brought the web down, and even then, it was only a matter of time before we were overwhelmed.

"It's time, Elspeth, *Liash li Ashli*," Mindel purred. "*Rise*."

I hesitated, struggling against the power within me.

Let me go. Let me go. Let me go.

"No…" I whispered, "I will not."

I was a Druid, and Druids could fold space and time. I could do the same in death if I chose. I'd draw them into death and imprison them in a pocket of reality.

It was a tough call, but it was only a temporary fix for a greater problem.

The Chimera wanted to kill and enslave everyone on Earth before moving onto their world, but still, I couldn't kill them. It wasn't a matter of not knowing how. It was about not staining my soul with the blood wrought by the black sun.

The veil wouldn't tear, not unless I screwed this up, which I wouldn't. There was no room for failure.

Kill them, the voice said. *It won't hurt. Not one bit.*

"No," I hissed, realising for the first time the truth of who spoke to me. "*I won't let you rise.*" I held out my hands and beckoned to the others. "I need your help."

"For what?" Vanora asked, her voice rising.

"I'm going to trap them in death."

"What?" Rory exclaimed.

"The Druids can fold space," I said, narrowing my eyes at Mindel who understood what I was planning. "Let's make the Chimera a new world. One where they won't be able to hurt anyone…and where no sun will ever rise." I looked over my shoulder at my family. "Will you walk into death with me?"

Unafraid, Delilah grabbed my blackened hand. "We are with you, Elspeth."

"*Tha sinn còmhla riut.*" Rory took my other. One by one, the remaining Druids formed a circle behind me.

"*Chimera!*" Mindel roared. "*Kill them all!*"

Swords held aloft, the vanguard of Fae charged.

"Whatever you do," I said, "*don't let go.*"

Colour bled from the cave as I called the veil over us, and death welcomed us with open arms.

Chimera slammed into the grey, the currents of death swirling around their ankles. The mist rose and wound around the startled Fae, halting their charge as colour bled from their flesh.

Colour flowed from the Elders and the Druids, making me a conduit for the fabric of reality. Death shuddered, and as the Elders worked their power through me, shimmering silver lines began to grow around the confused Chimera.

The prism flared, contracting as it formed, trapping the Fae in a pocket of death.

Mindel shouted at me, enraged. He snatched a blade from the nearest Chimera and rushed towards us, but we were too strong for him, and my command of death too absolute. The Fae slammed into the prism, falling backwards and convulsing as the mist drew him down.

I shuddered as the Colour began to burn my lungs and my throat scratched with shards of crystal, but I held on. The prison grew, encasing the enemy inch by inch until it snapped closed.

Crying out, I let go of the veil and the abrupt force snapped us back into life. The flow of power cut off and I fell to my knees, gasping for breath as death retreated.

Delilah knelt beside me, her palm rubbing soothing circles over my back.

"Is that what it's like?" Jaimie whispered.

"*O mo chreach*," Vanora rasped.

"Ignis…" I looked around for the cat and found him lounging on an outcropping of rock, licking his tiger paws.

"He's here," Delilah said. "His construct protected him."

"They're gone," Shor declared, dumbfounded at the now-empty cavern. "All of them."

"You did it, Elspeth," Rory murmured. "You defeated the Chimera—"

"No." I shook my head. "*We* did it. All of us together."

Rowen helped me to my feet, her touch soothing. "Can you sense any Fae who may still linger?"

She and Delilah held my arms as I let my senses ebb through the caves and into the tunnels. The Earth was silent, the Fae—

My gaze shot to a tunnel at the top of the cavern. "*They left something behind.*"

Jaimie readied his knife. "What is it?"

"Fire." I closed my eyes, my brow creasing as an unfamiliar sensation overcame me. "Shadow. It's twisting like a tornado…"

"An elemental soldier," Vanora whispered. "*Shite.*"

An elemental soldier? It was the same kind of creature that had murdered my father.

The Druids looked to the tunnel above us.

"How do we kill it?" I asked. "I always assumed my dad drew it into the bushfire and let the flames do the work."

"That's one way," Jaimie said.

"We deplete its strength and strike its black heart," Vanora told me. "That's the only way to come out of it alive."

"Or we run like hell," Jaimie added.

"We have to kill it," Rory said. "If we don't, it'll just come after us."

"It no longer has a master," Vanora added. "Without control…"

I understood. It had been bound by the Chimera and now it was free, and pissed as hell. Without control, it would wreak havoc and destruction, and not care who saw it or stood in its way.

An orange glow began to ebb in the tunnel.

"Are you well?" Delilah asked, laying a hand on my shoulder.

I grimaced as my stomach lurched with the after-effects of creating the prison. "I have to be."

"There's seven powerful Druids against one elemental," Rory stated. "We've got this."

"And one tiger," Delilah added.

Swallowing hard, I drew my knife. "It's here."

The elemental rushed out of the tunnel above, the air whooshing as flame tore around its body. Seeing us assembled below, it strode towards us with malicious intent.

I'd heard a lot about elemental soldiers from Rory but seeing one in person was a different experience than what was in my imagination. *Dad fought one of these? Alone?*

The Fae soldier was shadow wreathed in flame, its human-like features barely visible within its blackened skin. The elemental was fire personified; its magic drawn from the creation of life itself.

The creature was soundless as it approached, apart from the metallic ringing of metal on rock. It held twin swords in either hand, the tips dragging along the ground. The metal was so hot it glowed from orange to white along the length of both blades.

"*Liash li Ashli,*" it rasped in a guttural voice.

I stepped forwards, shaking off Rory's hand as he tried to pull me back.

"You're free," I told the elemental. "The Chimera don't bind you anymore. They're gone."

It tilted its head to the side. "You bargain for your life?"

"No," I said. "I'm offering you yours."

The creature began to laugh, an odd sound considering that it had no mouth I could make out.

"*Ash'an*," it said in its own language. "I was created to fight. Torn from the Earth for one purpose. *Ash*."

The soldier rushed at the Elders and they threw up their arms. The Fae collided with a wall of Colour and bounced back towards the centre of the cavern.

The web grew, forming a cage around us and the elemental. It would force it to remain here until it was powerless enough for us to strike—but that also meant we were locked in with it.

It seemed the elemental had made its choice.

I phased, blinking out of existence and reappeared behind it. My skin began to flake and crack as my Fae power threatened to take hold, and I pushed my Colour through the dark barrier, merging the two.

Lunging, I grabbed the elemental's wrist, my flesh hissing as flame burned my hand. Liquid crystal flowed over the creature's flaming arm and it roared in pain. I let out my own cry as I brought down my knife, the sound of crystal shattering echoed through the cave.

The sword the elemental had been holding clattered to the ground as the Druids circled us, ready to strike the next blow.

The Fae screamed out in an unknown language, its words garbled as its flame flickered and dulled. It swung its other arm, the second sword arching through the air in a crazed flurry.

I phased again, getting some distance, and crouched beside Ignis.

"*Liash li Ashli,*" it bellowed. "*Ash li 'an! Li ash' ashshri 'an ash 'anlili!*"

A stinging ache throbbed through my hand and eased as my power healed the melted flesh. I had a brief moment to be confused before the elemental resumed its frenzied attack.

It came at me, but Rory was there to draw its ire, his Colour joining with Jaimie's to syphon more energy. I hadn't seen them fight together before and now I saw why they usually worked as a pair. Their movements complimented one another perfectly, even though Jaimie was in his natural human shape.

As the elemental reeled, Vanora attacked from behind, casting a prism over it. The creature hissed as the holographic tendrils covered its head, forcing more of its flame to snuff out.

Enraged, the elemental swung its remaining blade in an arc, desperately searching for a mark to hit. The sharp edge slashed through the sleeve of Vanora's jacket, slicing her arm open. The Druidess cried out in rage and thrust her knife at the Fae's exposed side, her arm crawling with crystallised Colour.

The blade pierced shadowy flesh and the soldier roared, arching its back. Smoke billowed from its mouth as more of its fire died. Vanora tore the knife free, then stabbed it upwards and through the Fae's ribs.

She collapsed at its feet and her eyes widened as she began to convulse.

"Vanora!" Rory shouted.

He made to rush to her aid, but Jaimie wrenched him down as the elemental began to crack and bleed white-hot magma. Then, it exploded.

I threw myself down as the air burned, and Ignis leapt on top of me. The Elders held their web firm, the force of the explosion shaking the prism so hard, it rippled blue and white like waves in the ocean.

The moment the heat subsided, I wriggled out from underneath Ignis and rushed to Vanora's side.

Rory was already there, his hands smoothing back her charred hair. Ash from the elemental covered her from head to toe, her cheeks blackened by soot. Tremors wrought havoc on her body, her lips wet with foam as her eyes rolled.

I pressed my hand against her forehead and the Druidess moaned softly. She was cold, so very cold.

I peeled my hand away from her forehead and choked as I saw the smear of black on my fingers. *The veil.*

It wasn't just cold the Druidess felt. It was the chill of her soul slipping away.

"What is that?" Rory asked, watching me like a hawk.

I ignored him.

The veil rippled and reached out for Vanora's soul

and I shoved it back. *Not today. Not after she'd just saved us all.*

Laying my ear against her chest, I listened for her heartbeat, my Colour enhancing my hearing. The rhythm was easing, the time between each beat lengthening.

"Her heart is slowing," I murmured.

"The blade was poisoned." Jaimie cursed and tossed away the elemental's sword, the metal clattering across the cave floor.

I looked up at him. "What kind of poison?"

His brow creased. "The worst kind, lass."

The Elders stood over us, their expressions grave. If the three strongest Druids to ever walk this Earth looked like they had no power at all, then we had a big problem.

"Delilah, Shor, Rowen," Rory pleaded. *"Help her."*

"Colour cannot cure poison, Raurich," Delilah told him, her eyes misting with tears. "I'm sorry…"

"Elspeth." He turned to me, his eyes wild. *"Do something."*

"I can't bring souls back," I said, my panic rising. "I can only move them on. I—" My heart leapt. *"Dracaena Cinnabari."* The Dragon's Breath Osna gave me. It was still in my pocket.

Rory blinked. "Draca what?"

I didn't have time to care what Vanora or the Elders thought. Taking out the little vial, I grabbed the Druidess's cheeks, pried open her jaw, and dumped the Dragon's Breath down her throat.

Leaning over her, I pressed my fingers against her pulse. "C'mon, Vanora. You're stronger than this. Take it in. Let me help you…" I took her head in my hands and forced the veil back. "*Tha me còmhla riut.*" *I am with you.*

Then, all at once, her heart began to beat. Vanora's eyes flew open and she coughed, her hands grasping for something, *anything*, to hold onto.

"Ach! Vanora!" Rory exclaimed, taking her hand in his.

I said a silent prayer to Osna and fell back onto my arse, the exhaustion of all the fighting and phasing slamming into me all at once.

"We need to get her back to the Warren," Jaimie said. "The poison is neutralised for now, but—"

"She is deathly ill," Rowen finished for him. She knelt beside Vanora, helping Rory move the Druidess to a sitting position.

"I can phase us back," I told them as I wiped my brow. "I've got just enough juice left."

"Can you make it with all of us?" Rory murmured, taking my hand. "You used a lot of power."

I glanced at Vanora, then back to him. He loved her in his own way, I saw it now.

I nodded, feeling the *knowing* in my heart. "Yes, I can make it."

"Granddaughter," Delilah looked at Rory, Jaimie, then finally Vanora. "Rest. Now is time for us to look after you. After all, that's what family is for."

"Come," Shor said, reaching his hand towards Rowen.

My heart soared as the Elders opened a portal, the air parting to reveal a rippling doorway that would lead us home.

After all this time, after travelling halfway across the world to Scotland, I'd finally found what I was looking for. *Family*.

20

───────

I wasn't comfortable with being the centre of attention.

The moment I'd woken from what felt like a week of sleep, I snuck out of the Warren so I could be alone.

There was a lot to think about.

I sat on the top of Arthur's Seat, my feet dangling over the edge of the cliff. Behind me, tourists clambered over the rocks, desperate for selfies to commemorate the achievement of reaching the summit of the ancient volcano.

They couldn't see me through my illusions and, thanks to my strengthening Colour, I couldn't hear them, either. If you asked me, this was better than a pair of noise cancelling headphones.

Summer was at its height and the days still stretched well into the night. The Solstice had only

233

passed a few days ago and the sun didn't set until almost ten p.m.—the days didn't even get that long in Australia.

Rory sat beside me, his boots swinging next to mine.

I didn't even have to ask him how he found me. After all we'd been through, Rory and I shared a bond that transcended romance or friendship, even family. He *knew*, just as I did.

"How's Vanora?" I asked.

He didn't answer me at first. He just looked out over Edinburgh as if he was seeing it for the first time.

"Osna said the Dragon's Breath saved her life," he told me. "Vanora is furious she owes something to you, let alone her life."

"I wouldn't expect anything less."

I knew she wouldn't want any praise from me, but if it wasn't for Vanora, I didn't know how long we would've fought the soldier, or if we would have won at all. Her strike was the one that ended its life, almost at the cost of her own. If the Darkland Druids gave out medals, she should be the first in line.

"Where's Ignis?" Rory asked. "I haven't seen him all day."

I smiled and nudged open my bag—the same one with the blue beaded mandala Delilah had given me the day I left Edinburgh. A tiny ball of tabby kitten fluff was curled up inside, fast asleep.

"He must have had a hard life before he came to us," Rory said with a chuckle.

"He did, but what he's done for me and everyone since Delilah brought him back has been epic in its own right." I closed the zippier, leaving it half open so Ignis could climb out when he was ready. "I let him get away with pretty much everything."

We sat in companionable silence for a long time, soaking up the warmth of the sun, and the freedom of a Chimera-free city. For the first time in his life, Rory could enjoy the world above without fear of being hunted…so I let him enjoy every last breath.

He turned to me and smirked. "So, how does it feel to be a certified bad-arse?"

"Shut up," I complained.

"Six months ago, you were having an existential crisis every five minutes, now you're hacking off elemental arms, teleporting around the world, and facing off with hordes of evil Chimera. That's the definition of bad-arse, Elspeth. Don't shortchange yourself."

"It wasn't just me," I told him. "I am the sum of every person who has helped me along the way."

I was my father's daughter. I'd inherited his strength and level head. I had the knowledge of nature, given to me by Osna. I had the power of Colour, taught to me by Rory. I'd been given a warrior's heart by Jaimie. I had endurance and balance, gifted to me by Darby. I had tactical advantage, drilled into me by Vanora. I'd been gifted with language and insight by Delilah. And finally, unconditional love and friendship had been granted to me by Ignis.

Even Yenris'del had taught me something, even though her treachery stung.

There wasn't one hero in this story—we'd done it together.

"The Chimera are gone," Rory murmured. "That's all that matters."

I nodded. It hadn't taken the Darkland Druids long to figure out they'd all been called to the caves for the final battle. Even fake Mrs. Campbell had been there, though without an illusion, I wouldn't have been able to pick out which she'd been.

"There are still Fae out there," I said.

Rory snorted. "At least they're not an organised hate group."

I rolled my eyes, "They're not all Chimera."

"I know. We can't paint a whole people with the same brush simply because a small group decided to form a doomsday cult."

I snorted. Doomsday cult was a pretty good description of what they'd become. Now the Chimera who'd been trapped on Earth were trapped in a prison world inside death. Talk about drawing two short straws in a row.

"I had to do it," I murmured.

"I know," Rory replied. "You don't have to explain it to me. You did what you needed to do to stop the prophecy from coming true."

"The black sun spoke to me," I told him. "All this time, I thought it was my darker self trying to convince me to do evil things, then Yenris'del told me it was the veil. But in that cave…" I lowered my gaze. "It was the black sun all along."

"It's just a name. Nothing more."

What was the black sun anyway? Was it the name given to my Fae power or was it something that lived beside my consciousness like a parasite? I thought I understood what I was, but it seemed like I'd never know the full truth.

"I worry about Yenris'del," Rory said.

"She lives in her own version of hell," I told him. "Maybe that's enough."

"Maybe." He gave me a look that said if she caused any more trouble, the Druids would 'handle it'. "That fancy pants Fae called you *Liash li Ashli*. I wonder what it means?"

"His name was Mindel," I said. "He had better hair than Vanora, don't you think?"

Rory snorted and let out a small laugh. "She's also furious about having to cut off so much. That elemental took ten inches off her."

"I'm sure there's a prism for that."

My smile faded as a cloud skidded over the sun. I watched the shadow play across the city below, wondering where my future lay. The Druids had their home back and I was welcome in it, but there was still half of me that longed for the same thing I'd been looking for the day I walked into that travel agent's office back in Sydney.

Identity.

I shivered, despite the warmth. "The Chimera might be gone from the Earth, but they could still come back. They…"

Rory tensed. "They're still warring in your mother's world."

A mother I still wasn't sure was dead or alive. A mother I didn't know. A people whose blood I shared. It was a whole part of myself I may never understand —unless I travelled there the same way I came to Scotland.

"You want to go there, don't you?" he asked.

"While there are Chimera, the prophecy still lives," I replied. "It doesn't matter what reality they're in. We are the bridge, Rory. Our portals, and the ones the Witches guard, will always link us."

"But it's more than that, isn't it?"

I nodded. "I am Fae as I am Druid."

Rory smiled and knocked his shoulder against mine. "You have to know."

"I still have to ask permission. The Elders may not want me to stir up more trouble."

"Delilah will understand, and the others will, too. You've given us back our home, Elspeth."

I shrugged, uncomfortable with his praise.

"I can try to open a portal," he offered.

"My father didn't leave the address," I said with a

scowl. "There was no mention of it in his journal for good reason."

"So…"

I looked up at him. "We do this the right way. No more attempts at finding a needle in a haystack."

Rory pouted. "No more hellhounds?"

I laughed and shook my head. "Especially no more hellhounds."

"So, we're going Ireland? Cool. I've never been. Holidays aren't something Druids usually take, but now…"

My heart leapt. "What's this *we* business?"

"You really think I'd let you go on your own? I have questions that need answers and the Fae might know enough about portals to help us."

"To find the Darklands?"

He nodded. "One day, the needle will be out of that haystack and we will finally have our answer to the Druid's existential question. *Are we worthy of the homeland?*"

"If you want my opinion, then the answer is yes." If anyone was worthy, it was Rory.

"Your father thought we were," he added. "And if the heart of the daughter he raised is anything to go by, then his instincts are infallible. That means it's a chance I want to take."

My cheeks heated. "I'm not perfect. I don't know what will happen when I meet the Fae, or if the Witches will even let me cross."

"Aye, there'll be trouble for sure, but who doesn't love an adventure?" He winked.

"Do you think they'd be willing to forge an alliance?" I wondered.

"Who? The Fae?" Rory thought for a moment. "Perhaps. It's something we'd have to discuss with the Elders."

"Then we better start talking."

Rory smiled and shook his head. "*Tha me còmhla riut.*" *I am with you.*

Together, we looked out over Edinburgh and marvelled at the thousand years of history laid before our feet.

One world down, one to go.

"Ready?" Rory asked.

"There's just one thing I'd like to do before we think about Ireland," I replied, reaching into my bag.

"What's that?"

I pulled out the point of raw quartz I'd fashioned into a pendant with silver threads of Colour—which looked like sterling silver to human eyes—and showed him.

"Did you make that?"

I nodded. "It's a special gift for this amazing little girl I know. I owe her an apology."

He smiled and placed his hand over mine, adding a drop of his Colour to the crystal. The necklace contained some magic to make it sparkle with holographic blues and purples, but nothing that would invite danger. Rory seemed to think some green would round out the triad—an homage to the Druid's triple spiralled triskele.

"Don't be out too late," he told me.

I shook my head and rose to my feet. "I'll be back in the blink of an eye."

Then I phased, landing on the rocky shore of Loch Lomond.

OTHER BOOKS IN THE DARKLAND DRUIDS

by Nicole R. Taylor

Druids, **Witches**, **Fae**, and **shapeshifters** abound in this thrilling magical adventure!

Arcane Rising #1
Arcane Spirit #2
Arcane Mythos #3
Arcane Revenant #4

GLOSSARY

Scottish/Irish Gaelic:

**please note: the Druids deliberately speak the language in a more formal and pieced together way than fluent Gaelic speakers normally would. This is due to their nomadic heritage spanning across multiple worlds.*

- *dùin do ghob* - shut your mouth
- *bò bhrònach* - stupid cow (literal translation: sad cow)
- *muc salach* - dirty pig
- *neach-gleidhidh* (from Irish Gaelic) - guardian
- *a sheòid* - warrior
- *air do shocair* - take it easy
- *stad* - stop
- *O mo chreach* - good heavens / oh my goodness
- *tha sinn còmhla riut* - we are with you

Fae Language Glossary:

- *Liash li Ashli* - roughly translates to 'goddess of death'
- *Ash li 'an! Li ash' ashshri 'an ash 'anlili!* - You will die. I don't believe in your prophecy.

- *ash'an* - never

ABOUT NICOLE

Nicole R. Taylor is an Australian Urban Fantasy author.

She lives in the western suburbs of Melbourne dreaming up nail biting stories featuring sassy witches, duplicitous vampires, hunky shapeshifters, and devious monsters.

She likes chocolate, cat memes, and video games.

When she's not writing, she likes to think of what she's writing next.

Follow Nicole Online:

Website: www.nicolertaylorwrites.com
Facebook: facebook.com/nrtaylorwrites
Newsletter: www.nicolertaylorwrites.com/newsletter
Email: nicole.this.is@gmail.com

ARCANE MYTHOS
(THE DARKLAND DRUIDS - BOOK THREE)

Witches guard the way.
The Fae hold all the secrets.
And a woman from another world has three
days to stop a devastating war...

Elspeth Quarrie has embraced her powers and her new name, **Odhweine**, and defeated the greatest threat the Druids have ever faced.

They are safe for now, but the fanatical Chimera are destined to return as long as Elspeth's prophecy holds power. The only way to ensure her new family's safety, is to travel to another world and end the threat once and for all.

To reach the Fae Realm, Elspeth and Rory need to win over the Witches, and once they do, they need to win over the illusive Fae Queen. It isn't easy being a harbinger of death, especially when all Elspeth wants is to save the world...from herself.

But when the portal takes her somewhere unexpected, Elspeth finds herself in the fight of her life.

For the end of all things will begin in Un Alari... unless she can stop it.

***Arcane Mythos** is the third book of **The Darkland Druids**, a mystical Urban Fantasy series set in modern day Scotland, Ireland, and the spellbinding world of the Fae.*

A powerful woman, who is the embodiment of death, travels to another world in order to save it…from herself. Can she stop a devastating war from sweeping across a magical land? Find out in this gripping fantasy saga!

Want more novels just like this one? Check out Nicole's other series:

THE ARONDIGHT CODEX - An ancient war with demons. A lost sword with the power to end it all. And a woman with purple hair is the world's only hope.

THE CAMELOT ARCHIVE - Set in the same alternate Arthurian world seen in **The Arondight Codex**… Deadly secrets. Murder and revenge. The end of the world is nye and Camelot is the last bastion of hope.

THE WITCH HUNTER SAGA - Vampires and witches collide in this thrilling Urban Fantasy adventure. You've never met vampires quite like these…

THE CRESCENT WITCH CHRONICLES - Witches, shapeshifters, and ancient myth collide in this colourful Irish flavoured series! Come on an adventure fraught with danger and forbidden romance… and the ultimate battle to save magic before it's gone forever.

THE DARKLAND DRUIDS - A woman with no living relatives travels from Australia to the other side of the world to find out the truth of who she is…only to land in the middle of a prophecy of destruction. Druids, witches, fae, and shapeshifters abound in this thrilling magical adventure!

Find out more at: NicoleRTaylorWrites.com

See what titles are FREE at: Nicole's Free Reads